The
392

Ashley Hickson-Lovence

First published in the United Kingdom in Hardback by:
OWN IT! Entertainment Ltd

Company Registration Number: 09154978

Copyright © 2019 Ashley Hickson-Lovence

Ashley Hickson-Lovence has asserted his right under the Copyright, Designs and Patents Act 1988 to be identified as the author of this work.

Cover design: James Nunn

Hardback ISBN: 9781916052307

All rights reserved. No part of this publication may be reproduced, stored in a retrieval system, or transmitted in any form or by any means, electronic, mechanical. photocopying, recording or otherwise, without the prior permission of the copyright owners.

WWW.OWNIT.LONDON

For everyone who takes the bus

"How tightly packed in we were on that bus platform!
And how stupid and ridiculous that young man looked!
And what was he doing?"

        Raymond Queneau, *Exercises in Style*

NATALIE

Hackney born and raised, I grew up on the street, the block, the bits, the estate, the hood, the ghetto, the ends, the manor. Whatever you wanna call it, it's up to you innit, but it was a total shithole, something from a book, and not one of them fairy tales because I ain't no princess. So now I'm writing it all down, every little bit, using the notes on my phone so you can read all about it.

Keep calm you know? How can he text me to keep calm? I could kill him. I feel to go to his flats, through the playpark with my hood up, wait for someone to buzz me through the big blue doors, *my auntie lives on the fifth floor and her intercom doesn't work,* climb the concrete stairs two steps at a time, squeeze in through his mum's kitchen window, creep into his bedroom – like I've done bare times anyways – and while he sleeps, shank him again and again. Boy, he's just lucky I'm not the violent type.

I mean, what must I look like? Standing here under a

railway bridge that stinks of piss, stroking my belly, which ain't even that big yet! How can he send me a message saying I should keep calm, allow him, and leave him alone? Not even man enough to come and say something to my face and accept the fact he's gonna be a dad soon. Not man enough to come to this first proper appointment today – see our baby for the first time on the little TV and check we're well and healthy. Not there to hold my hand as the nurse puts that proper cold jelly on my belly, or get my phone from the bottom of my bag to take pictures to put on Insta, ask the doctor questions and all that stuff dads should do.

It's cool though, he'll see. I'm sick of sneaking round his mum's anyway, slipping off my new 97s in the passage and tip-toeing upstairs into his room like some cheap sket. I don't need him. My mum raised me on her own and my nan raised my mum on her own too. I haven't seen my dad since I was like seven, and I don't need to neither. Anyways, I'm kinda lucky in a way, at least my wasteman babydaddy never gave me no STD like my girl Bethany's man; got myself checked out at the Ivy innit, just in case. Got the all clear.

If people ask, my Facebook name is Miss Princess Natalie Amelia Nathans and I have 523 friends. In the education section, I've put I went to the University of Life, because even though I'm only nineteen, I've been through bare shit. And I could have gone to University Metropolitan Southbank of something if I wanted, because I done a BTEC in Health and Social Care once and I nearly got a Merit. I'm learning now though. Deleting him right here at this bus stop: Insta, Snapchat, Facebook. He's dead to me. R.I.P. Prick.

Trust me when I say that wastemen like him are like buses. Shit. I've been waiting for this route now for like four, five weeks and still no sign of it. Not waiting at this bus stop obviously, I'm not thick, but I saw a poster a month ago about this new bus going from Hoxton to Highbury and I thought, with the baby coming and that, I could take this to Highbury and then get another bus to Whittington for all my scans and stuff. Whatever happens, I don't want my baby being born in Homerton though because that hospital is dirt. My baby might not have a dad, but I don't want them catching no disease like Ebola or bird flu or that Zika madness.

The bus stop is packed. Bare buses have come and gone but no one wants the 67, 149, 242 or 243 today. We're all waiting for the same bus to turn the corner and pick us up and take us where we need to go innit. Everyone must want to get on this new route and go somewhere different, try something new, go on a little adventure all round the back streets of Hackney. I mean, who doesn't like trying out new things sometimes?

True say though, I have to say, it's always changing round here. Shops that used to sell carpet cleaner and cat toys, now sell those tiny espresso coffees that are too strong and make your breath kick so you have to buy chewing gum straight after. I remember when it used to be really rough round here, with gang fights between Hoxton and London Fields always going on. But now, all the white men wear big girly hats and them skinny jeans so tight it squashes their nuts and them 'Doctor Martins' – or whatever they're called – and thick cardigans and even thicker glasses that make them look older than they really are.

Not even sure if I like this new Hoxton though. How many coffee shops do we need? And why my gonna pay like four bills for a tattoo down Pitfield, when my girl Destiny can come to my yard and do it for fifty? Don't get me wrong, I like that I don't have to pick up my Pizza Hut from New North Road anymore, because the delivery driver was too shook in case he got robbed. And cabs actually come into my estate as well these days, because before they didn't. But there ain't no kids left in the park, no ball games, no fun.

Finally, just in time before I get vex, I can see the bus's little face at last. The 392. It's turning the corner so slowly like it's too shy to meet all of us for the first time or something. We all move closer to the edge of the pavement, all of us: a blind man with his white stick, a young black man in a grey suit, an older balder black man with a big black kitbag, a white man in a blue suit, me, a crackhead, a tourist-looking man looking lost and a brown man with a big beard and a rucksack. I clock them all. I remember from my days watching *Crimewatch*, it's important to be observational sometimes innit. Especially in times like these.

The 392

I haven't seen many women bus drivers, especially black ones, but this one's kinda pretty rocking that colourful headwrap ting, even though she's got a big jawline like one of them violin players or something. She's smiling but her face looks a bit oily and sweaty like she could do with a baby wipe. She looks nervous like she's only just passed her test and is scared she might crash.

The bus is busy already, but there are a few seats free. Don't really like sitting near the front because it usually smells of old people and them foreigners but I don't feel like sitting at the back either like I used to. I'm not that sort of girl anymore. I did think about getting one of them Baby on Board badges to put on my jacket, but that's a bit bait, don't really want the world knowing my business. I choose somewhere near the middle and get my phone out straight away, I've got a story to write.

There are lots of important-looking people in suits and ties, chatting and smiling and looking out the window at the sights as if Shoreditch is some fancy place in New York. There are people taking pictures and a cameraman wearing a bomber that says BBC London on the back and filming all sorts of shots. He's moving like paparazzi. I swear, they better not film me. Luckily, the camera is focusing on some politician sat at the back I've seen on the TV once. One of them posh people that don't care about us black people being forced out our own homes by hipsters rocking them chunky platform kreps that were dead a decade ago.

I look out the window like it's a film I'm watching. There are signs that say *Hackney is a 20mph zone* and there are people about to take out those Santander bikes that you can borrow for a few hours to get to work or school if your bank card hasn't been blocked. The man with the beard and rucksack that looks proper heavy gets up from his seat and it's not even a bus stop. He nearly falls because the bus shakes a bit as it turns left to go towards the market and clips the kerb. Maybe he knows the driver. He looks a bit lost and is fiddling with something I can't quite see, something it looks like he's trying to hide. I mind my own business though because this is my story, not his.

It smells like dog shit on this bus; the crackhead has shat himself and we all know it. When people get on, they sniff a couple times, then look around with a scrunched face like, *what the fuck is that smell?* The crackhead probably doesn't even know he reeks because he's just sat there on his own, all calm and relaxed like he's thinking, *what a lovely day it is*, looking out the window. He's talking to himself so loudly like he's being interviewed by someone when no one's even bothering him.

Another block has been knocked down, the street stripped bare like a sket. There'll be nothing old left soon. That's another building gone; will the others make it? The roads of

Hoxton are small; the driver makes the bus bounce off the pavement as we go past the gym and the car park. Roadmen doing GCSE retakes look at us like they want to either fight us or chirpse us, standing outside New City College with their hoods up and screw faces. Their heads go from left to right like CCTV cameras as we drive past.

The Lion Club looks bare different these days. There are loads of flats but not many houses round here. Over there is the estate. The same like it was back in the day. It's always weird going past all those memories, like them times playing *ip dip dog shit*, and feeling nervous because we was swearing for the first time and worried that our West Indian mums might hear us. Especially when we said the *fucking bastard silly git* part. These were the days in the ends before it got rough as fuck.

The playpark behind the estate was a warzone. The older boys, who we called 'olders', had special uniforms – these long black coats that covered their whole body and faces, except for two big spaces where their eyes were so they could see out. It kinda looked like they was wearing gas masks. And these times, footballs flew about like bombs, you had to duck all the time when riding your bike round the playpark in case you got taken out by what the boys called a 'Ronaldo special'. When it started to get dark, angry parents gave orders from balconies. Sometimes, olders gave you commands too like they were sergeants. It was mad. It was a no-man's-land if you weren't from the ends, but it was cool though, because I knew people innit. And now it's my duty to get all this down quick before my battery dies – this memoir could be a bestseller like *Harry Potter* or that *Fifty Shades of Grey*.

Some loud schoolgirls get on and disturb me from my memories of the ends, laughing and chatting so loudly like they want all the attention on them. I eye them up as they both sit down right behind me like they deliberately want to piss me off, and I try to concentrate back on my writing. They better not try and start anything. They best not mess.

I remember them red nose pitbulls on short chains growling bare loudly at everyone all the time, saliva pouring out the corners of their wide mouths like hot and cold taps. The wannabe MCs spat their latest bars in the park when the sun went down. You had to use the light from your Sony Ericsson to see their hooded faces all lit up. Spit would literally be flying out their mouths as they rapped, and their big fat pink lips vibrated like... vibrators. Their rhymes were so clever though, it took you a few seconds to get what they were saying, because sometimes you didn't even realise that they were slyly cussing people. People you knew as well.

And one time, one of the olders came to the ends with the latest camera phone wanting to make a video for *Channel U* with some girls in it to make himself look like one of those players on TV like Aggro Santos and Nu Brand Flexxx. And you really wanted to be one of the girls to make it in the video.

So they would ask you to make a test video at one of the older's flats and you had to strip off all your clothes, basically, and dance to some grime tune so they could see if you was good enough. They would call you a whore if you tried too hard, so you had to get the balance right and only whine your waist a certain way at a certain speed, and not lick your finger too much while they filmed you. We never did see the finished videos on TV.

Them days were mad though. The lifts in the estate was always some next drama. You never pressed the buttons with your fingers because it was dutty. You had to pull down your sleeve and poke the buttons with your thumb through the cloth. And sometimes there was a big puddle of piss in the lift and you never knew whether it was the stinking piss of a pitbull, a little Turkish 'younger' or a crackhead. You had to stretch one leg over the big puddle to the other side and stay stretched across till you got to your floor. And when the lift was broken and the intercom door wouldn't open, you had to stand tall and act brave because the hoodrats sold weed on the stairs. Even though I was a girl, you had to say 'cool' to them still and run past quickly or they could jack your phone or the P you was saving for chicken and chips. And there was only ever just enough for a chicken and chips, but because the bossman behind the counter knew us from time, he always chucked in another hot wing for free, on the sly.

For fuck's sake, I don't think I can take this much longer.

From behind me, more loud chatting of shit, I'm getting proper vex now. These schoolgirls are so extra, they're properly starting to get on my nerves. Making so much noise, when I just want to get all this down before I get distracted and forget it.

'Tyriq likes to stick it in round the back,' the lighter-skin schoolgirl is saying. 'He says it makes him cum harder.'

'Estelle! That's disgusting! How do you clean it up when he's... you know?' the darker-skin girl asks.

'You mean cum? Johnson's baby wipes obviously! Duh! I thought you were the smart one Di.'

I take a deep breath, fake a cough and turn around.

'Sorry,' I interrupt, 'but could you be a bit more quiet please?'

Their two faces turn to look at me; their mouths open so wide I can see the dangly bit at the back of the throat. They kiss their teeth at the same time, then just ignore me and carry on chatting.

'Do you mind keeping it down?' I say again slower, getting vexer.

There is an awkward silence; some of the passengers are looking. Then, they both start laughing so loud, like they can't stop. Louder and louder by the second. I stare at them harder, longer, stronger till the lighter one says:

'Come Di, let's move from this waste chick, there's two seats near the back.'

And like that, off they go, stomping to the back of the bus like two skanky dogs that have been told to piss off by their owner. As we head towards Dalston, the driver puts her foot down like she's the female Tyrece from *Fast and Furious*. We're speeding like she needs to go McDonald's or something before they stop serving the breakfast menu. At the front of the bus, the man is still standing there, with his heavy-looking No Fear rucksack over one shoulder. As we bounce over another bump, a blind guy to my right gets to his feet and starts swinging his stick all wild in his direction. He's waving it about like it's a machete. The man at the front doesn't move. It looks like there's something big in his bag, something that's been stuffed in and is about to split wide open.

RAY

I've never been on safari before but I've heard lions roar, 35,000 of them in Cardiff back in 04. Millwall vs. Manchester United at the Millennium Stadium, both teams fighting it out to win the oldest and greatest football competition in the world, the FA bloody Cup. I remember it like it was yesterday: the boys in blue complete underdogs, rank outsiders, the no-fucking-chancers. It bloody showed. The game went as expected, the might of Man United overpowering us boys from south London. Ronaldo, class, Scholes magic in midfield, Van Nistelrooy, clinical. Final score: Millwall 0, Manchester United 3. In truth, we made it far too easy for them. Didn't close them down. Didn't get tight enough. Showed them too much respect. We got battered, and in more ways than one. It's not the last football match I've been to, but it was the last one I ever saw.

Me and the boys made a weekend of it, drove down in a minibus on the Friday and hit the streets of Cardiff that night: pub, bar, club, cheeky stop at a strip club, didn't catch a wink of sleep. I tell ya', we were proper smashed by kick-off. It didn't matter though; we had belief, the magic of the cup and all that. And what a decent team we had: Lawrence, Wardy, Marshall in goal and the danger man from down under Cahill (and I suppose Ifill and Elliott weren't too bad either... for coloured lads). On our day, I really fancied us; anything could happen in ninety minutes. And to be fair, we held out until just before half-time but then they overloaded the box and Ronaldo nodded it in to the corner to make it one-nil at the break. It was all one-way traffic after that.

That wasn't the worst of it though; the next few days were the dark days. Sitting in that hospital bed, battered and bruised, barely breathing and not knowing whether the doc was a sheepshagger, a nigger, a paki or a chink. My family all around me like it was my deathbed they were surrounding, or worse, my coffin. Turns out, after the final whistle, as I went for a tinkle down this little alley round the corner from the stadium, I was jumped on by a pack of dirty Mancs who didn't like the look of my face, the cut of my jib, the lion logo on my top. The coppers asked what I remembered, and I told them what I knew: seven or eight of them, one of me. It was a stampede. It was like I was Mufasa from *Lion King*, only I didn't actually die. Looking back now, I wish I did. I was totally outnumbered: nutted and robbed, punched and stamped on. I've had a few tasty punch-ups in my time but these cowards fucked me over good. If I were to ever see them again...

I'm sat next to a fucking crackhead; I can almost taste it. All that shit and piss and sweat, my body fights the urge to not smash this fella up for stinking out the bus. I can picture his stinking piss around his crusty cock. The sweaty folds in his skin. His threadworm-infested shitty trousers. It's all mixed together like a fishy fucking stew that's long gone off. The bus itself smells new and almost like plastic but add it to the stench of my crackhead mate here, it all comes together to create this weird mix that don't sit right in my gut.

I don't wear shades like that Edgar Davids because I can make out odd shapes. Faint outlines. Blobs. And I still know these streets like the backs of fists; I've done The Knowledge. This journey so far: Kingsland Road, left, Falkirk Street, right, Hoxton Street, left, Crondall Street. I could do the whole route. Back in the day, I used to live on Haberdasher and strut down Hoxton Street wearing wallabies and barging into people, thinking I was Richard Ashcroft in the *Bittersweet Symphony* video. I remember every turn, every twist, every jolt of this massive city from seventeen years spent behind the wheel of my old black cab. From Peckham to Putney, Tulse Hill to Tottenham, New Cross to Charing Cross: celebs, royalty, broads, I drove them all, and heard all kinds of stories I tell ya'. Had all sorts going on behind my back too: blood, sweat and semen – affairs, pregnancies, strokes, heart attacks. The lot.

The 392

Hoxton at heart, I went south of the river every Saturday to get pissed on the Old Kent Road, wear Reebok Classics and feel fucking free for a few hours. Football fan or not, everyone knew about us. *Nobody likes us and we don't care!* we chanted from the stands. I loved it. I was attracted to the aggression straight away, the pints, the passion, the possibility of scars. My first game was Yeovil away. Nearly got nicked before kick-off.

Now asking 'who's that?' all the time is getting me down. Every day is the same. I have to sniff shit out first like a dog, and I don't know what I snort up my hooter. On a night out, I could be pulling a pig and not know it. I don't even know what I wank to. I have tattoos I can barely remember: a faded lionhead on my neck and the names of my children on my wrists but I don't see 'em much these days no more. I strain to remember their faces but looking into the past is like trying to see through cling film.

Pissing hell, hurry up! This bus hasn't moved for fucking ages. I've got an appointment at the Laycock for nine forty-five. Dr. Richardson, she's young and white I'm told, proper sweetheart, English too (I made sure of that). Ow! What the fuck's going on here then? Something hard jabs my foot. Then again. Harder.

'Excuse me, who's the blind one here?' I ask.

'Sorry love,' an older voice croons, whacking my leg again trying to get through with a shopping trolley or Zimmer frame or something. She pushes and pushes and squeezes through eventually, it seems, as the bus starts moving again. The crackhead leans in close. The smell of him worse than before somehow.

'Do you like football mate?' he asks.

Even though I can't see nothin' but colours and shapes, I look down at the home shirt that I'm sure I put on this morning and turn to face him again.

'No,' I say, hoping he gets the hint, tryna get out the conversation early doors.

'Rugby?'

'No mate.'

'Cricket?'

'I'm not big on sports to be honest, mate, I'm blind,' I say.

'Oh, right you are,' he says so casually.

There is a short silence and I shift about in my seat to try and get comfortable somehow, I can hear it's beginning to rain.

'...Muslim... bomb... bag, ya' know?'

It's him again, the smelly crackhead cunt. 'What's that mate?' Unable to hear him with all the bloody racket of some schoolkids at the back and tryna not get too close and breathe any of him in.

'There's a bomb in there... I bet ya'.' He slurs his words like he's sunk a few Special Brews already this morning. 'You got 40p, mate?'

The 392

The bus snakes on. Is this dickhead crackhead fella trying to tell me there's a bomb in some man's bag? Like a bit of bad gear my heart feels funny, all tight like a clenched fist, blood not flowing proper as the realisation slowly sinks in that if this fella is right, we could all die in a minute. I mean, nothing surprises me anymore, all you ever hear these days is terrorism this, terrorism that. Can't even get on a bus to see the GP without the risk of being blown up by a rag from Pakistan. A rag we probably let into this country aged eight and kept well fed with British benefits. It's a fucking joke. It's basically our taxes paying for their B&Q bomb-making equipment! And what do we do? Put bloody barriers on bridges. Is that the best we can do? I tell ya' what we need to do, build big barriers round the whole of this island, starting down in Dover. A big fat fucking wall. Trump's got the right idea.

I've had enough; I need to do something. Blind or not, I can't just sit back and let this happen. What was it Bowie sang? *'We can be heroes'*. I feel us turn right into Downham Road and as the bus straightens up, I stand. *'I, I will be king'*. I'm clutching my stick tightly and humming. I'm on my feet now and edging forward in the direction of the man at the front, towards this geezer who apparently thinks he's bomby big bollocks. I'm pounding my chest. I am a lion. *'Just for one day'*.

LEVI

Feral rioters stripped shelves bare in minutes across London in an orgy of looting in the capital. From groceries to clothes to electronics, high streets in Clapham, Hackney, Dalston, Peckham, Woolwich, Lewisham, Enfield, Walthamstow and Tottenham were ransacked. Initially targeting mobile phone shops and sportswear outlets, youths caught up in the thrill of criminality filled their arms with loot and fled into the night. Everything imaginable was stolen. One youth even posed with a large sack of Tesco Value Basmati rice, proving that items need not to be valuable to be targeted by looters.

Daily Mail, August 2011

Don't know why I still do it, torture myself like this, punish myself this way. Don't know why I still carry it around with me, among the files in my satchel. I can't lie, those summer days were dark days to be a Londoner, days best forgotten, but I can't help reading this same article over and over again.

I was lost for a while. I must have asked about a dozen

people what bus I needed to get to Highbury Corner from here, but it seemed barely anyone knew their own area. I asked a guy with a camel coat, shiny head and bushy beard; the young Chinese couple; the pretty pair, matching skinny black jeans and Stan Smith Adidas trainers; a man with a man-bun and denim three-quarter lengths. None of them could help me. Not when it came to buses anyway. Some suggested I jump on the Overground from Hoxton but I don't like trains, too scared of getting derailed. I finally found the stop I needed after circling the area for ten minutes or so, maybe more, and managed to catch this little 392 bus around the corner from New City College, who are, judging by their large purple banner, very proud to have recently been graded *Good* by Ofsted.

I overhear people getting on say that this route is new, which probably explains why it's already pretty packed. As I squeeze on through the single-set of doors at the front, nodding to the smiling bus driver – black person to black person – I notice a mixture of passengers already sitting, standing, chatting and mincing. I shuffle past a nervous figure with a rucksack slung over one of his shoulders and swing into a free seat.

This area is an attractive one, no doubt about it. And the council are clearly trying to make it nicer, with building work taking place on every other corner. The building site to the left is alive with activity: a swarm of yellow hard hats buzz about, grafters wearing Lonsdale trainers and paint-stained Slazenger tracksuit-bottoms yell at each other in harsh Eastern

European tones from opposite sides of the site. *Considerate Contractors* boards and *Safety on Site* signs. Crushed Tyskie cans in back pockets. It's all happening; foundations have been dug-up and re-laid.

There are pairs of good-looking couples clutching coffees and shiny MacBooks, smiling Colgate grins. They wear Puma hoodies and neon Nikes with skintight bottoms that make their legs look fit and firm. As the bus takes a tight right turn and pulls into a bus stop opposite a building marked University of the Arts London, I notice two cool fashion types – students from that institute presumably – puffing on roll-ups and wearing green loafers and extra-long, extra-large puffer jackets. A hooded boy walking a staffy and carrying a bulging side-bag shuffles through their smoke uneasily.

I know what's going on. It's happening in Tottenham too. Tottenham ain't 'Totty' no more. I've seen the new big breweries and the coffee shops as you climb out of Seven Sisters station. I've clocked the quirky art installations and the proper posh chicken shops that sell real certified chicken they market as 'healthy'. There are new flats everywhere and new types of people moving into the area with their bowl-cuts and tortoise-shell glasses. I've seen the hipsters in tie-dye t-shirts taking modelling shots in Markfield Park. Even the football team are getting in on the act of fixing itself up, White Hart Lane doesn't look like it used to. I remember when Bruce Grove was a proper shithole; you can't imagine what it looks like now. And even the Jews can't afford to live in the area no more; they're packing their boxes into the back of their Toyota people-carriers and heading off to Canvey Island with their ten kids in tow. In many ways, I think I'm getting used to the changes I'm seeing daily. I feel safer in the area now than I ever did growing up and I can't lie, I'm partial to a soy chai latte from Starbucks every now and then, especially if I'm working on a difficult case and need the caffeine to keep me going. But I see this influx of hyper-fashionable millennials – the people who protest about the state of the environment and the academisation of local schools and the over-development of the High Street, and wonder what will happen to the heart of N17 in, let's say, a decade or two.

I dust off my blazer and trousers, straighten up my tie, check the time and wonder how long this journey will take. I remember watching *The Apprentice* when I was younger and knowing I wanted to have a job where I could wear the sharpest suits and nicest shoes. I didn't want to be a businessman on that show though, because I didn't want to sell raw fish down Ridley Market one week and design a dating app for geriatrics the next. I didn't want to have to say *I'm so ruthless, I would sell my mum to make a profit*, get fired for being a shit project manager in the first week and have to say *Thank you for the opportunity Lord Sugar* watched by millions of viewers. So I decided that that life wasn't for me. I had to think of another career where you could look smart and not be a cunt.

Man, look at me, today is the start of a new chapter and I've got to make the most of it. This is the beginning of a new journey, literally, with new people on board: the crazy guy pretending to take pictures, the mixed-race girl, the lost-looking tourist at the front with his bag on his back, the camera crew, the blond-haired politician at the back, the driver, everyone. At the start of this new November day, we might as well try to enjoy the ride.

But these nerves, I just can't shake them off. As we get closer, the memories come flooding back. It was tense in there that day. Those magistrates weren't in the mood to mess about. They'd presided over similar cases all day, so when it was time, well, they were probably tired and wanted to get the job done quickly. I could see their mugs of coffee and swollen bags under their eyes. There were three of them. One old white man sandwiched in-between two old white women. Boy could that man talk; he went on and on.

'You are charged with the offence of common theft on the night of Monday 8th of August 2011,' he started saying. *'It is reported that on this night, you stole one 10kg bag of Tesco Extra Value basmati rice from the Tesco superstore on Tottenham High Street. You then proceeded to post a picture with the stolen goods on your Facebook page with the caption: 'I'm gassed. Dinner sorted for the next month.' You took advantage of a tumultuous time for the city, on a difficult and hostile night in the capital. Your actions were deplorable, notably in the aftermath, flaunting your loot on social*

media. Having heard the case against you by the CPS, we hereby issue you with a community service order of 180 hours and a £200 fine. It is hoped that you can repay the community that you clearly set out to destroy with your unscrupulous actions.'

And just like that, it seemed all over.

The female magistrate chipped in.

'Do you have a closing statement, sir? Any last thing to say for the record, Mr. Brown?'

There was a big pause.

'Well... Whatever innit. All you've done is chat a load of bull to me from the start, but what about Mark Duggan and his family? Where's the proof he was carrying a weapon? What about the officer who shot him? Why is he not here facing charges and made to look like some fool like I am? What about how them police treat us in Tottenham? Just look what you're doing to Broadwater. The system is trying to break up our community. You can't knock down my home. Our homes... Your honour. Your honours. Why punish me for trying to feed my mum and younger brother?'

'Mr. Brown... Mr. Brown...,' the middle magistrate kept trying to interrupt, but the tirade continued.

'This is meant to be my hearing but you're not even hearing what I'm trying to say... you lot clearly don't feel our pain, man.'

Despite the emotional closing plea, the case was done. Finished. Ushered out by a member of the court security staff through a set of doors at the back.

* * *

This journey is a bumpy one. We pass a caged tennis court and another block of vulnerable old flats. As we get closer, the memories come flooding back. Still can't quite believe I'm going back there today: Highbury Corner Magistrates' Court. Me. Levi Brown: basmati thief to budding barrister.

GLORIA

Small packet of mince, one potato, some cheese, greens, half a loaf of bread... and maybe a sweet, enough for a last supper. Or should I sod it all? Get one of those fancy ready-meals? Something to heat up quickly and save all the fuss. None of it will matter anyway, dear, I won't be hungry anymore the day after tomorrow.

All these aches and pains, it feels like I've been through the wars. I wish I could wake up for once and not feel sore all over. I wish I could sleep at night and not suffer from shooting pains, crippling headaches and a nagging numbness. I wish it didn't feel like pushing my little trolley might finish me off good and proper. It's taken me at least ten minutes to get to this bus stop and every minute hurt.

My knees aren't what they used to be, dear, it's tender around the cap. Tendons are tired and ligaments all worn down and sore to bend. It's often too difficult to go up and down stairs and sitting too long makes it almost impossible to get up again. The pain throbs harder than my heart, but I'm too old to be fixed now. Even the doctors know I'm damaged goods.

It's another one of those tired London mornings, one that feels like the tower blocks might topple over on top of me and I could be crushed at any minute. I keep my head down to escape this biting breeze, because the heavy grey clouds hang low today, like they're getting ready to burst under the pressure of it all. I sensed it as I cut through the back of the estate. They're trying to terrorise me and I let them. I'm almost relived to experience one last overcast London morning, before it all comes to an end.

I have today's timetable clear in my head: it's up to Dalston now to do a last little shop using the new bus. I will take it to Dalston and crawl up to Ridley to get the last bits I need for tonight. I know where I need to go. The leaflet put through my door the other week told me. I know this bus goes all the way to Highbury Corner, but I don't need to go that far, there's no one waiting for me up there.

Doing the shopping used to excite me. Hunting out the best bargains, scrimping and saving my pennies to get the best deal down the market, but these dark days are different. Now I have no one to cook for. There was always a hot plate ready when Al got in from work, and even if he didn't say, I know he always appreciated it. Appreciated me. It'll be two years this Christmas since he dropped dead, bless his soul.

The 392

I must say, truth be told, this new bus is good for the area really. My little Hoxton is getting way too big and busy and the 394 is always too full. I miss how it used to be: The White Horse, Hoxton Hall, the Iceland that used to be a Co-Op, Britannia Leisure Centre, Dad's Barbershop, the little bits and bobs shops, Cooke's pie and mash, the old library. Everything has changed. I feel like a foreigner. The language of the kids is unfamiliar to me now, and I don't even recognise many of the buildings anymore. There are weird smells everywhere like I'm in a completely new country and I'm breathing in foreign air. It's as if I live in my own old bubble that is shrinking every day, making it harder and harder to breathe.

Now, it's all runners and rubble, *CAUTION! Demolition in Progress* and puffer jackets without the sleeves that say The North Face; and Hoxton Street Monster Supplies and schoolkids scoffing chocolate biscuits and washing them down with fizzy pop; and young Orientals in weird clothes; and mobile phones and roadworks and men kissing men and Europeans carrying tools in big Sports Direct bags. The streets aren't safe. I was nearly run over by a runner the other day. Everyone round here is always running. Who are they running from? Where are they running to? And I don't understand today's fashion either. There are big holes in people's jeans like they've been ravaged by a pack of foxes. I can see their knees! Why would anyone choose to be colder on a chilly day like this?

People rush around with satchels and backpacks, clinging to them, as if they're clutching all their hopes and dreams inside. The world moves so fast. Where are they rushing to? Who needs them this early?

Me.

My skin has lost all vigour, all life. There is no product that can restore the colour. There is no serum that could make my skin taut again. Some days I wish I was chucked into an asylum or diagnosed terminally ill, at least then there might be someone for me, a reason to visit. Neighbours, friends, family, they've all disappeared down the years, their voices a faint whisper in my ears. Now all I have is the memories, but even these are starting to fade.

It's never been easy, I had to leave Ireland young. Both my parents drank and bullied me blue. Picked on me for being the youngest and ugliest of the family. I remember once, during bedtime prayer, being tickled by my sister as father knelt with his head down and his eyes closed. Unable to hide my giggles, I was punched for the sinful act of blasphemy. My older sister laughed while I sobbed and sobbed, cowering from my father's ready right hook. There was only so much I could take. At the first opportunity, aged eighteen, I ran off to London, lived north of the river, south of the river then settled in the east. Married Al; became a nurse. Retired.

I still remember the howls that echoed through the hospital as the bed-ridden screamed long into the night, regretting their drinking and drug taking and sleeping with people they'd only just met in noisy nightclubs. It was a kind of suicide really. When they saw me start my shift, they would try to force a smile from across the ward to get my attention, wanting me to come and keep them company for a while. They knew I always would too. For many, their friends and family didn't want to know: too ashamed and embarrassed of the life they had chosen to live. I heard all their sad stories. They squeezed my hands urging me to help them in some way, save them from the constant pain they were feeling. But there was nothing I could do for them then, the damage was done, I was just there because no one else was. It was too late for the poor things. Their bony fingers clawing into me, digging into my skin with tears filling their eyes. I remember them getting paler and paler, thinner and thinner by the day as the disease got into their bones. I feel like they did now.

My only daughter lives abroad, Valencia I think it was last. With two little ones, my grandchildren, two little boys, twelve and five, who probably prefer their other Spanish granny than me. Who probably don't even know I exist. They might visit if I was dying. Instead, they are far away, near a beach somewhere where the sun is probably always shining. When I was young and able enough to manage airports and aeroplanes I used to visit them on the coast. Now, all that queuing and fuss with heavy luggage at the gates is too much for me.

I'm too far behind the times to catch up now. I'm old-fashioned and unwanted. I don't own a mobile phone that can take pictures and play music. I don't have a computer so haven't joined the estate community group on Facebook. I've never had the shopping delivered to the flat. I don't drink fancy coffee from one of them fancy shops down the market, far too dear for me. I used to feel important now I doubt anyone would notice if I dropped down dead tomorrow. I was once the star of a snap, now, I'm shocked by own reflection: the lines, the bags, the split-ends, the dead-ends.

Just as it starts to rain, here the bus comes, all shiny and new like most things round here these days. *392 Highbury Corner* it says on the front. Bouncing over the bumps, it slows to a stop by my feet. The driver lowers the bus for me using a special button and opens the doors. I edge forward and use all my strength to haul my trolley onto the bus, which I just about manage with a struggle. I'm in but I'm exhausted already and my pocket is empty. Where's the blasted thing? I always keep it here. This pocket here. It's not in this one either. Or this one. It's not in my purse is it? It shouldn't be. My pocket is empty. *Sorry*. I've lost it. Everyone's watching and I can't find my pass. It's gone; it must have fallen out when I was walking through the estate. I won't get that back now. *I'm so sorry*. I feel all hot and useless. The driver, a young black girl whose eyes are big and brown and is wearing a lovely colourful headwrap, seeing me get all flustered and getting myself all in a panic, looks over her shoulder quickly and waves me on anyway, as secretly as she can. I nod her a *thank you*, at least someone is nice to me.

This bus is warm but smelly. There is a cameraman filming. There is an almighty racket at the back, schoolchildren of course. I dare not look for long. The young show no respect to us anymore. There is a strange man speaking to himself. There is a stranger man at the front with a bag filthy with dirt that reads No Fear. I hear the word 'bomb' said by someone. I don't know whether I should be more scared than I am already.

I squeeze past him; my trolley has me in tow. There is a man already sitting in one of the priority seats. He doesn't look like giving it up either; men aren't gentlemen these days, not like my Al. My arms are getting worse. I can barely move this trolley any further. I push and I push but the wheels won't move, I'm stuck, I'm hitting something...

'Excuse me...' A voice says. 'Who's the blind one here?' It's a man with a faded blue sports jersey that says Ryman on it. He's holding a blind man's cane.

I feel myself get red and all I can get out, all stressed and flustered and still feeling pathetic and useless is, 'Sorry love.'

I find a seat. After a second or two, wiggling my trolley as close to me as possible, trying to not get in the way, and gazing out the window into the new modern world, I feel the slow trickle of a tear run down my cheek. By the time I taste its saltiness my mind is made up. Enough is enough; I've become a blind man's joke. There's nothing left, there's no one left. It's time to call it a day. I'm staying on, and when I get to Highbury Corner I'm going to do it. I'm going to make myself feel better. I'm coming Al... my sweet.

STU

Did I hear her right? *Thank you gorgeous*? Now these are words I weren't expecting, words that take me by surprise and catch me off guard completely. It's true, I do feel particularly sexy today, it's just, you rarely see bus drivers smile, hear bus drivers speak, and certainly never find bus drivers who are so ruddy fit themselves.

There is a strange pause following this remark. I smooth down my curls and straighten up my shoulders. Her pleasant smile and my surprise meet as my card finishes its bleep and my heart stops its beat. The fogie in front fumbles with her purse, having barely made it down the aisle, giving me an extra few seconds to have a good look. She, the driver, seems amenable and meek. Someone who clearly feels it's their duty to thank you for paying the obligatory £1.50 fare, when actually, the pleasure is all mine. I should thank her for looking so beautiful, for making my morning, for restoring my faith in true black beauty.

Her profile, striking: soft edges but a strong jaw. Her eyes coffee-coloured, an indulgent Douwe Egberts blend. She waits patiently, not wanting to close the doors and set off until everyone is seated. She has a heart, clearly. She holds her smile as she glances up at her little internal mirror to see what's causing the hold-up. Her nervous grin grows. Quite a queue is forming now because the granny is still struggling to put what must be her pass back in her purse, and then her purse in her bag, and then her bag in her shopping trolley. Other drivers would have activated the automated voice already that orders passengers to *please move down inside the bus*, but not her, not my beautiful black anomaly.

I use this delay to study her hard. I'm awestruck by her magic. Her dark skin emits a tropical warmth, and it's late November. She exudes exoticness, a portrait rich with colour: from her floral headtie, to her eyes, to her skin. I'm already getting all hot under the collar. The softness of her face makes it hard to distinguish her age, she could be in her twenties, she could be forty. It's hard to say (I hear they age well). As is the question of her name. Why don't bus drivers wear name badges?

There is an innocence about the way she sits, a shyness that I like, a sexy stoicism that I want to explore. She has this aura about her, like she's the type that would actually wait for a person running for the bus in a hurry, or allow a slow

Nissan Micra through at the other end of the road, despite the pressures to keep to the timetable.

My thoughts race on but I find myself awkwardly positioned at the front, squashed against a man with a bag with little room to wiggle free. Little progress is being made with the old lady and her shopping trolley, who has now managed to get one of her wheels stuck on something. I use this opportunity to peer through the perspex and work my eyes down the driver's body. I wish her hands that grip the steering wheel tightly were gripped around my waist instead. She has painted her manicured nails a steely teal. I wish they were digging into my bare back. I wonder what she's wearing down there. I can't see below her waist. I wonder if she's all tucked in, all neat and tidy. I wonder what her bum looks like. I wonder if it's peachy. I uncontrollably lick my lips.

Right. Change of plan. No work today. I want to take the District Line with her to Kew Gardens, go inside that old glass building and see the African plants that remind her of her African childhood. I want to marvel at the androgynous orchids, both phallic and vaginal. Take the Overground from Kew to Hackney Wick. See a show at The Yard, drink red wine and pale ales till last orders. Or, get off at Haggerston and see if Duke's Brew and Que is still open and get the ribs that are too big even for the two of us to eat. I want to take her away from New City College and Crondall Street and crackheads by the chicken shops. I want to look after her, supplement her meagre bus driver salary with whatever I earn. I want to rip off her uniform, tear at her navy V-neck, fling off her headtie and ruffle her hair. I want the next leg of our journey to involve her legs around me. We could go back to mine, a little drunk, and shag till sunrise. Or even, if she's keen, just fuck right here on the backseats of this bus when we get to Highbury.

I imagine her naked, her brown tits rubbing up against my pale freckled skin. It could be our disgusting little secret. We'll be so sexily discreet that no one will see us. And because the bus is new, we won't even have to worry about the seats being too dirty because we'll be the filthy ones. She'll spank me raw, wearing her leather driving gloves (I bet she's got a pair). I want red streaks across my buttocks. I want specks of blood on my bum.

Fuck it. I won't get off at Dalston, I'll tell the office the traffic was heavy, or there was an accident or something and make my move on her instead. All this Crossrail 2 proposal work will be going on for months, years, one day off won't make a bit of difference. Everyone knows it's a good idea, TfL don't need to pay me to confirm it. She needs me.

But it seems bus drivers are destined to be alone. Take the classic Routemaster, the bus on mugs, posters, t-shirts, tea towels and Cath Kidston holdalls. The driver had their own little compartment at the front, separated from the passengers and conductor. Left alone to wrestle with the steering wheel before the days of proper power-steering. It shouldn't have to be this way for someone so important.

It's busy. The blockage on the aisle has cleared and I'm nudged forward by pushy passengers behind. There's a funny stench in the air, I can smell it worse now as I edge forward. I don't stray too far down; I want to be as close to the driver as I can. I find a seat quite near the front; close enough to keep my eyes on the prize.

With a jolt, we are off finally. I heard there would be a camera crew and the rumours about a certain MP making an appearance were true. This could be a chance for me to brown-nose with a bigshot, but right now I can't take my eyes off her: so strong yet still so slender and sexy. She's concentrating hard now, checking mirrors and blind spots routinely, masterfully. But her smile has faded and I bet it's because of *him*, this man at the front. I know his game. There's something about the way he looks, the way he stands, the way he dresses, in his baggy jeans and rucksack with something in his hands I can't quite see properly that I don't like. He shouldn't be competition. I mean I'm not usually the jealous type, haven't needed to be – look at me – but seriously, what is this guy playing at? She should be mine for the taking. But why is this man with the bag so determined to beat me to it? We pass Shoreditch Park to the left and I've got my eye on him. The creep.

DIAMOND

'Be good today, you saw how Mummy was this morning.'

'I will, I will...'

'I mean it Kamari, no more fighting with that Alfie boy.'

'He's so annoying though!'

'Kamari, listen to me. I mean it.'

'OK, I won't, I won't, *jheez Loo-eeze*,'

'Give me a kiss... Kamari! Kiss!'

And with a quick peck on my cheek, off he goes, zooming his way through the school reception like a plane being flown by a drunk pilot. His arms stretched out wide, book bag swinging from his wrist, through the automatic doors and bouncing out of sight towards the Year Five classroom of Mr. Cook. I haven't been inside 5B yet this year, but I can imagine what I would see: pencil pots, Pritt sticks and papier-mâché, scraps of coloured card, tissue paper, ridged borders and laminated work from the *Pupil of the Week*. Book trays with everyone's name on. I miss the days when life was as simple as sitting on the carpet for a story, school dinners and Golden Time.

Mum is really sick, and this time it feels worse than before. I haven't told Kamari yet, but I'm not sure she'll make it to Christmas, and I'm still not sure what will happen to us when she's gone for good. I knew it was bad when she told me what the doctor had told her a few weeks ago, but I haven't had to deal with something this big before, and I'm not sure how I am going to cope when she's gone.

My mum is a proper black woman. Jamaican and proud. She kisses her teeth (some gold) when annoyed, she shouts down the phone when she's not even angry and she's still sort of offended by gay people (or 'batty men' like she calls them, but she's getting used to them because of her love of *Queer Eye*). But she's not been herself lately, and it's clear that the illness is starting to take over. She just sits at home in her dressing gown in front of her TV in her bedroom watching repeats of *The Real Housewives of Atlanta* and *Dinner Date* on ITVbe.

Since the illness, apart from watching TV all day, she only has enough energy to drag herself to church on Sunday. She tries to pretend everything is normal, strolling in smiling, greeting everyone with massive hugs, wearing her big hat, in her best church dress. But when she thinks I'm not looking, from the corner of my eye I see her coughing blood into a tissue, which she hides in her bra, and sneaking out to the toilet to probably be sick between hymns.

'Are you OK, Mummy?' I would whisper when she wobbled back.

'Of course, my child,' she would say as if angry I asked, 'I'm in the house of God.' And she'd slide into the congregation's singing of *What a Friend We Have in Jesus* as if nothing had happened.

I wonder how many church services she has left.

For the first time this year, I am going to be really late for school. But today, having seen Mum this morning, pale and weak and vomiting into a little bucket by her bed, I don't even care. I won't tell the teachers about her illness, I don't want them or anyone to know and then feel sorry for me. And anyway, what would they do with me and Kamari?

I walk fast in my old Kickers and skip through the leisure centre carpark. It says 09:11 on my phone so I hurry to meet Estelle. My new background wallpaper is a picture of a picture. It's Mum holding Kamari in the hospital bed at Homerton and me next to her looking at him like he's the most beautiful thing in the world. It's my most favourite photo. I must have been six and I look so happy in my Dora the Explorer denim dungarees.

I kinda jog past the bicycle shop and the betting shop and up the little hill with the water running underneath. I'm meant to be meeting Estelle by Regents Canal at quarter past so we can get the new bus to school together. Estelle wants to 'mark her territory on it' she said on WhatsApp; I still don't know what that means, but it sounds like a bad idea. She'll be mad that I'm late to meet her, but won't care we're gonna be late for school. Even though we've officially started our GCSEs as Year 10s, she's still that same girl that I went to primary with, starting fights with girls she don't like, kissing her teeth at teachers, kissing boys. She might even get kicked out soon.

It's my birthday next Thursday, my fifteenth. I have just a few impossible wishes: I wish Mum wouldn't die, I wish Dad would visit more, I wish Kamari's dad would see him more. And more than anything else right now, I wish I had a boyfriend.

The wind feels good on my face when I run and nicer on my eyes. My contact lenses are a bit burney this morning. They're all dry and sore but Estelle says boys don't like girls in glasses unless they're white, so I bought these purple lenses in Ridley Market last week for a fiver. They take me ages to put in in the morning, and it's even harder when your eyes are so watery and red already. It really hurts actually, and the other day one of them got stuck in the back of my right eye; for about five minutes I was so scared I was gonna go blind forever. But I trust Estelle when she says it will help me get a boyfriend; she's the smartest person I know when it comes to boys. Anyway, I'll probably get laser eye treatment when

I'm older; Estelle says you can pay for the surgery in monthly instalments.

Typical. When I get to the canal, all out of breath and about to die, Estelle's not even there. She's probably still styling her hair in front of the mirror singing along to Mabel. While I wait, I look down into the dirty green water where the canal runs below and see bits of Walkers crisp packets and old Coca-Cola cans that have turned brown and rusty. The drizzle causes ripples. For a moment, even though I can't swim, I wonder what it would be like to jump down and let the water take me somewhere new. Maybe I could end up in Essex or somewhere nice like that. As I bend over, looking for my reflection in the slosh, I am pushed over and caught at the same time by the hands of a slender teenage girl. Estelle Winters. Her hair is brushed back into a bun that kinda looks like a bagel and she's wearing her white Nike socks pulled all the way up with her navy-blue Lacoste sliders that her mum bought her from BooHoo. Her skirt is folded over at the top to show off her shiny baby lotion-fresh legs. She's definitely a bad influence but she's definitely beautiful. She's popular with all the boys because she's mixed-race and everyone knows mixed-race girls lose their virginity in Key Stage Three.

The new little bus comes just as Estelle finishes hugging me as an apology for scaring me and it starts to rain properly. We get on all loud and giggly, talking and taking the piss out of random things. There are lots of people on it already, there's even people filming, but luckily there are two seats in the middle that are free so we race to them. I spot a boy in the very backrow, slightly older, on the phone staring at us like all those other hungry boys out there like to do. He's got his hood on but I can see his purple and black Grove tie, or City of London Academy or whatever it's called now. Estelle likes the attention but it makes me feel uncomfortable when boys look at me like I'm a piece of chicken from Nando's. I suppose it's something I will have to get used to though, if I really want that boyfriend one day.

This bus is so stupid. We go around Dalston train station in a circle for no real reason. Nobody gets on or off and Dixy is closed. Estelle told me south Londoners think Morley's is better than Dixy but they smoke too much weed down there so it messes with their head. Everyone knows Dixy is the best. It was Sam's for a while but I think Dixy is the number one chicken shop again, just ask the Chicken Connoisseur.

'I'm glad we're leaving Bregsit... I don't even feel safe in London no more after what happened to Jermaine.'

'That was nothing to do with Brexit, Estelle.'

'Yeah, I know! But Polish people smell innit.'

'Estelle! You can't say things like that!'

'You know I'm right, look at that skanky man there, I bet he's a terrorist.'

'Estelle!'

She really has no idea about the world, but as I sit here

and look at him properly, I can kinda see where she's coming from. Standing right at the front of the bus, right by the driver, acting a bit strange is a man with a rucksack and one of those beards that people who live in Whitechapel have. He was standing there too when we got on. He looks nervous and uncomfortable like he's lost or something or maybe Estelle's right and he is a terrorist and there really is a bomb in his bag. Anyway, terrorists were definitely not to blame for Jermaine's death. We all know who that really was, but we can't talk about it... snitches get stitches and all that. We all cried and cried when he was stabbed near St. John's. Sometimes life isn't fair.

When the bus goes over the humps it feels like when a plane flies through a cloud. The bus turns right onto a small road with lots of posh houses. A road that no other bus travels on because there are no proper bus stops. I guess people just have to ring the bell if they want to get off, or put their hand out if they want to get on. The houses on this road are really old and beautiful, very different to the block of flats we live in with the rubbish chutes, and broken lifts and drug dealers parked up outside in their Mercedes. I wish to have a house like one of these one day, they must cost over a million pounds. I bet it would have a big garden for Kamari to play football in and a good-sized kitchen and sitting room for a massive TV. I want the best for Kamari. I don't want him to end up like one of those Hackney roadmen on street corners, calling out to girls, wearing a full tracksuit even when it's boiling hot. I don't want him to be a part of the Fellows Court Crew and the other gangs around Hoxton.

Estelle is always trying to advise me about boys. I wish I was a bit more like Estelle. A free spirit with no respect for the normal rules of society. I like that about her.

'I had some good sex last night Di.'

'Estelle! Not on the bus.'

'You gotta just lay back and let them do their thing. Tyriq likes to stick it in round the back. He says it makes him cum harder.'

'Estelle. That's disgusting. How do you clean it up when he's... you know?'

'You mean cum? Johnson's baby wipes obviously. Duh! I thought you were the smart one Di.'

I laugh, sort of disgusted, sort of jealous, but don't dare to ask any more questions.

A woman who is sitting in front of us turns around and says something as we crack-up at the thought of Estelle wiping herself clean.

'Sorry... but could you be a bit more quiet please?' the woman says, quite politely actually. She's older than us, pretty though.

But Estelle pauses, looks her straight in the face, shocked she had to cheek to breathe and then kisses her teeth in a really loud long way. I copy her exactly, movement for movement, sound for sound.

'Do you mind keeping it down?' she says again, slower and angrier, but Estelle just ignores her and starts laughing in a really loud and exaggerated way. I do the same and start laughing my head off too, looking at her to make sure I'm doing it exactly like she is. Maybe this public rudeness is what Estelle meant about 'marking her territory'.

Straight after, Estelle grabs my hand, like a true leader and says, 'Come Di, let's move from this waste chick, there's two seats near the back.' So we stomp away to create a scene for everyone to see.

Now we're both listening to Ayo Jay's *Your Number* on my phone because Estelle doesn't want to waste her battery before school. We have an earphone each, with the volume low enough to still talk and hear things going on. We're gonna be so late but it's always fun going to school with Estelle though, I can't lie. We talk about everything: boys, school, sex obviously (she's winning this last one seven-nil). The boy sitting behind us – who we've been showing off to on purpose without actually speaking to him – pokes his head in-between the both of us. He pulls down his hood and strokes his chin.

'So, what you sayin', you gonna give me your Snap or what?' he asks, turning his head to face me directly.

'Pardon?' I reply, shocked he's chosen to speak to me over Estelle. Beautiful light-skinned Estelle.

'Insta then?'

Has my birthday wish come true a week early? This could

be like *Love Island*. Maybe this boy – fifteen, sixteen, with the cute smile, fresh shape-up and combed-out afro hair – could be Kamari's new dad. One he has never really had. Even after Mum goes there is still hope we can be a proper family like the ones you see on *Don't Tell the Bride*. Or like one of them posh couples that have just moved to Hoxton and go for Sunday walks to the flower market in their fur coats and Ray Bans, holding hands and drinking coffee... but I've got to slow down, play it cool. I look at him all shy.

'I don't just... give my personal information to any random boy on a bus, how do you know I don't have a man? You don't even know my name.'

'Look listen, I'm a big man round here you know?'

'Oh yeah?'

'OK then. What do you go by, sexy?'

'Do something for me and I'll do something for you. You see that man over there, standing near the driver? My girl Estelle here says he's a terrorist. If you're such a big man... save people. Be a hero.'

Estelle looks impressed by my tactics. She nods and smiles and in her head I know she's saying *Is that you, yeah, Diamond?*

'What?' the cute boy says.

'Oh, I thought you were a big man?'

He tries to change the topic and asks why I'm late for school and says I look like a 'good girl'. Whatever that means. With Estelle's support, I tease him a little flirtatiously, licking my lips the way she taught me to do. Next thing I know, I find myself calling him a 'pussy' for not being brave enough and that's the trigger. Just like that, off he goes, down towards the front of the bus – followed by a chubby blond-haired man – his trousers hanging down low showing his boxers, ready to prove himself to be a potential father for Kamari and maybe even a child of our own one day. Let's see if he passes the test.

BOXER

'Oi cuzzy, what's going on, you heard? Big news bro, my brother got his ting pregnant. Yeah fam it's mad. Proper mad. Mumsy's mad vex, says she's gonna send him back home. She's saying I'm the last hope in the family now. Me you know? It's a joke ting. I know fam; your world can just change just like that. It's mad. Blackz was like, maybe we can pass round her mum's and stomp on her belly. Yeah, trust, it's deep... He's pissed though, 'cos she says she's keeping it... The mum? She's had a rep since Year 7. Remember that sket from ends fam... Nah, not Leshante bro... Nah, that's Briana... that one lighty that used to live in Colville with the nice breasts. That Natalie chick... Yeah. Her.'

This is actually serious; it's a human baby we're talking about. I don't think she's really a sket either but once you have a reputation in the ends, no matter how unreliable the source, it's hard to get rid of it.

'It's mad though, never thought the situation would end up like this... I swear, this bus is so wavey man, can't even go in a straight

line, gonna be bare late for school. Fam, it's going all round the ends in some mad directions, should of got 271 still. It's bare bumpy too. What? Yeah, proper busy. It's actually a proper shiny new bus as well, not even got dirty chicken boxes underneath the seats yet, or Sharpie graff, it's just got all them posh man on it. Seriously though, what's the ends coming to? It ain't what it used to be. Yeah, I'm basically in Dalston now. Yeah I'm jamming at the back innit ...'

I lower my voice, nearly to a whisper.

'There's a man on here, I think he's that politician bre, swear I've seen him on TV before, the one that doesn't rate black people or immigrants. That guy with the proper yellow hair that's always mad messy. Yeah him. I think that's why there's a camera crew on here setting up innit, allow getting baited out on TV man. Don't even have a bally on me like Unknown T. Not feeling being on London news today.'

Although saying that, being on TV might be kinda nice to be honest. Might even help me get a nice girl if I get exposed and they see me looking peng.

'Fuck's sake... I hate buses. This one is so small, it's like a flipping van or something. I swear my aunt's whip is bigger than this titchy ting. I feel like my personal space is being violated. Driver looks like a proper auntie too, she's got gold earrings and one of them colourful headscarf tings like she's going to church for a wedding or something. Not gonna lie though, free travel is bless still. Do you remember them days on them long 149 buses, jumping

on with Fleeks, and Chucky and them lot? We used to just jam at the back, bussing jokes and playing music out loud on our phones? We used to slip into other ends bare as well, but no one would ever try a ting on us 'cos we had a mad rep them times. We used to go all the way to Edmonton Green for no reason, remember? We used to proper violate that free travel and then jump off when we saw the inspector 'cos none of us used to carry our Oysters with us anyway.'

I remember causing so much stress for members of the public for no reason. I actually always hated it.

'Watch when I pass my test though, gonna go all round Enfield, Walthamstow, Leyton, all them ends there, trust me. Oi have you seen Jamz's Snaps? He's going in. That guy is some pagan, baiting out skets. I've been bussin' up though, that guy is bare moist, outside Westfields you know? He went in. How can man go Westfields without any P though? That's some joke ting. I seen his vid this morning, bunnin' a spliff before school, that guy's not serious. Anyway, mad props to you though bro, I hear you're doing bits... Yeah? Cool, cool.'

He wants to hang up now, I can tell. It's my friend Joseph; he's ghosted to Watford now. His mum said he was hanging around with the wrong crowd in Hoxton. I need to keep him on the phone till I get to school. I don't wanna look like I'm all alone.

'Yeah, I'm gonna be bare late. Don't even care; these teachers take the piss. I just wanna slap their backheads so badly, Grove has

changed bare since back in the day. You heard it's an academy now? Bare wasteman teachers thinking that they run tings these days, it's some joke, Sherman was a wasteman too, always running up his mouth with his dead kreps. He's gone now though but swear down, if I saw him on road, I'd dip him in his face.'

I obviously wouldn't.

'Real talk though, I need a new job... huh, the one I got now? That job's shit bruv; they need to start paying me more dough. They be treating man like a modern-day slave these days, it's a pisstake. Fuck zero-hour contracts man. But G anyway listen, you gotta be bare careful in block these days. You heard Scrapz got six years? Yeah man, feds found food in his Audi. It's deep. The feds are proper tryna clean up the ends these days. Oi G, there's a lighty on this bus you know, some Highbury Fields chick, kinda, looks like she's got a nice backy. Yeah yeah, she's got on outside T's block, with some other chick. I might have to move to that still... They're coming to sit right in front of me now.'

But oh shit! Is that? Oh man, this is bad. I've just seen... sitting at the front, it's definitely her isn't it? It's Natalie, my brother's babymother. Didn't even clock her before, even though it's a face that shouldn't be hard to miss. She looks so sad holding her belly tight like that. This is bad. Maybe I should I ring Blackz and Chucky, get them to do their plan and maybe Mum won't send my brother back to Nigeria? I should allow it though really. She looks broken, like she's been crying all night. She's proper vex at my brother, you can tell. It's written all over her face like a Post Malone tattoo.

'Yeah man, I'm still here, listen G, I gotta go. Need to save my battery for school innit. Yeah cool, holler at you later, we'll go chill in studio or something, I'm hearing Kabz has been working on some sick new beats... yeah, yeah, cool, later...'

I cut him off, I need to concentrate. Natalie is still looking out the window like she proper regrets her life choices – like she wished she could turn back time. In the light, the little bit that comes through the window, she's looking peng still; she has such a nice colour to her skin. It makes me think that I would do anything for a proper girlfriend. How deep my brother must have been to her for the situation to end up like that. But nothing could ever happen between us, deep down I know that, loyalty and family and all that, so I might chat to these girls instead, see if they're on it, see if they wanna be with me. I take a deep breath and randomly tap the left one – the darker one on her shoulder as she chats loudly to her friend about something unimportant.

'So,' I start proper confidently, 'what you sayin', you gonna give me your Snap or what?' You gotta be bold with these feisty late-for-school types.

She slowly takes out her earphone from her ear and turns round to face me. 'Pardon?' Her eyes are purple and her face looks decent, kinda sweet.

'Insta then?'

'I don't just...' She pauses to choose her words bare carefully. 'Give my personal information to any random boy on a bus, how do you know I don't have a man? You don't even know my name.' I wish she said 'boyfriend' instead of 'man'. She speaks like the rest of the road girls around here, which is a little bit of a turn-off. I want someone smart and well-spoken and ambitious to be my girlfriend. I carry on anyway, for the fun of it, feeling braver.

'Look listen, I'm a big man round here you know?'

'Oh yeah,' she says. Her and her lighty friend find this funny and both start laughing sort of loudly, some of the other passengers look back kind of annoyed. I carry on the game, feeling I might be in here even though inside I'm not really on it.

'OK then. What do you go by, sexy?' She smiles a bit when I say this.

'Do something for me and I'll do something for you,' she says kinda sexily, licking her Vaseline lips bare slowly, either her or her friend smells a bit like that pink baby lotion stuff.

'You see that man over there, standing near the driver?' She nods in the direction of a man with a beard and a dirty bag on his back. He looks kinda Turkish or something, like one of them men with the long knives from Hoxton Best Kebab. 'My girl Estelle here says he's a terrorist. If you're such a big man...' she says, looking me dead in the eyes, 'save people. Be a hero.'

'What?' I'm kind of shocked at how this conversation has developed, I now need to risk my life to impress this girl I've only just met and not really that into.

'Oh, I thought you were a big man?' she says like she's offended.

'I am,' I say kinda weakly. 'Why you late for school anyway?' I ask hoping to take the heat off me a bit. 'You look like a good girl.'

'Had to drop my little bro at his school... but anyway, don't change the subject, go speak to that man, you ain't no pussy are you?'

You ain't no pussy are you? Wow. The cheek.

'Me? Don't get it twisted. I told you already, I'm a big man out here.'

Before I even realise it properly, I get up to go down towards the front of the bus kind of fake angry, kind of scared too. This girl's got me properly wrong. I'm not really like that, one of them always-starting-trouble sort of street boys, but I feel like I've got to do something now, like I've got a point to prove. The politician guy with the messy blond hair has got up too and is behind me heading towards the front of the bus like he's going to back it. I walk with a fast bop down the aisle because that's how I should walk in front of people: past the men in suits, and some guy writing something – a poem perhaps – in his notebook. An old granny has kind of blocked the way with her shopping trolley and the blind guy with his white walking stick thing nearly whacks me on my legs. Then, someone grabs my blazer, hard, I'm about to switch as my hand closes into a fist, when I clock who it is. Of course it's her.

'Boxer,' she says. It's Natalie. Up close, she looks absolutely amazing.

BARNEY

Time to mess it all up. Northern Line it. Ruffle this High Barnet good and proper. The more unkempt the better; I can't be looking neat and normal after all these years, I need to give the people what they want and if that's a bumbling buffoon with bad hair, then that's what they'll get. Today is a big day, a day that could put *me* in the driving seat, so there mustn't be any hairy surprises.

To start, Hoxton.

A few customary *hellos*, a smile for the camera here, a handshake there and a scramble on board this tiny bus. I head straight for the back but before I can get comfortable we're off, swinging around the dizzying backstreets of trendy Shoreditch, through rough-and-ready Hoxton estates, old and new, riding the humps towards Highbury like a Crossrail train on newly-laid tracks. There are more new-builds sprouting up on street corners, arty students in double denim and Doc Martens, clusters of trendy coffee shops and cafés. To the right there is a strong single market, but one that is only open on weekends it appears. What's for sure though is that the Overground has done its job in putting Hoxton on the map. It feels alive.

I've been told the roads are too small for a spanking new Routemaster; that would have been campaign gold. A shiny new London RM, conductor and all, going around the backstreets of gentrified Hackney would have been glorious. But crikey, these roads are so tight, like being in a Land Rover inching up towards the National Trust house at the top of the narrow lanes of a Devon seaside town. Hunter wellies and Barbours; unpredictably driving rain one minute and picturesque bright sunshine the next. This driver seems to be handling the challenge well enough for the moment though as we weave our way northbound.

This journey is a much-needed escape; I do not feel at my best today. I needed to clear my head, shake off the headlines: referendums, remainers, reshuffles, Article 50, hard borders, backstops, single-trade agreements, transition periods, taxes and tariffs, formal negotiations, Chequers, temporary customs agreement, more cabinet reshuffles, expensive divorce bill, votes of no confidence, withdrawal agreement and political declaration. What a mess! I have no idea what our future will look like.

They've picked a woman driver for the occasion today. A black one too, that's a Brucie bonus. This will look very good on BBC London with Riz later. I just hope there are no hiccups, no crashes, no crushing of any cyclists because the media would have a field day. No one is allowed to die this morning. Though I must say our captain looked competent enough when I got on: clutching the steering wheel with a pair of strong hands, wearing a wide smile and bold colours, a little nervous obviously, but she needn't be worried, all she has to do is get to Highbury without killing anyone.

I bounce about at the back over every big bump as we turn into another side street. While at the front, stands a figure with a backpack. He's been there for a while now. He sort of resembles a young Sadiq but taller and sporting a big unkempt bushy beard. I don't think he's saying anything to the driver, just loitering, fiddling with something in his hands.

I'm struggling this morning, it's killing me, more so than ever now, I'm dying for a snippet of Skepta, or a touch of Tempa T to lessen the tension a little. I'm getting all hot and sweaty, waiting, paws on knees, to be summoned by the TV crew so I can be interviewed and get this all over and done with. I can see they're still getting it all ready and set up. Interviews make me nervous, despite all the experience in front of the camera and constant media training. There's so much at stake, and your every word can be so easily misconstrued. I just have to keep calm and repeat the same rhetoric: runways, referendums and remaining. I just hope I don't accidentally blurt out something I shouldn't, or reveal that my true passion isn't housing, or education, healthcare or foreign policy, but in fact... grime music.

It's ridiculous, isn't it? There's always the daily danger of accidentally blurting it out. It is my deepest and darkest secret; I can't let the press find out at the risk of tomorrow's papers reading: *Barney is down with the kids but down with the voters*. I don't want everyone knowing I cycle into Westminster listening to Kano or that I sing Skengdo in the shower. It's a deep-rooted worry, but even now I'm desperate for my next fix: a smidgen of Stormzy; a dash of Dave; a sprinkling of Sneakbo. I'll even take the faint sound of a passing car blaring out some J Hus. I have the itch. I feel the sweat spreading across my brow. My insides feel numb. There is an empty ache in the pit of my stomach and I just need some grime to take the edge off. Thank Christ it's a quieter day today: simply answer some questions, mention Crossrail a few times and I can be on my way.

The unsavoury male is still dallying near the driver. No one seems to be giving him much attention at the moment, but he's certainly making me more unsettled. He stands there clutching the straps of his rucksack tightly. Switching nervously from looking at the driver to the camera crew behind him, then on the road ahead. More so than ever, I desperately need some AJ Tracey and Fredo to rid this angst.

Dalston, I've got to know it well.

There's that Haggerston pub, busy bar downstairs, birthday

venue up top. And that shop selling cacti plants, Prick. Despite protests, Passing Clouds has closed down. The 76 no longer goes down Stamford Road. The shop (not) selling (social mobility) scooters is still there in the corner, so is the Oxfam. And there's Creams, seems London has gone dessert diner crazy. The camera crew have yet to sort out their equipment. We whizz around the bus station at the backend of the not-so-new-now Dalston Junction station. To the right, I spot the narrow doorway of what was Visions, the underground nightclub that played a healthy dose of decent music till six in the morning, I've heard. How I would have loved to have gone for one night, start pre-drinking at home with a couple of bottles of Captain Morgan's, stuffing Kettle Chips in my gob to line the stomach. Jump on the Overground with a Coke bottle full of rum, wearing a baggy Fendi tee with skinny black jeans, Gucci belt and pair of Balenciagas on my feet. Name already on the guest list, an alias of course, so I get to jump the queue, which snakes around the corner towards the front of the Overground station. Get an inky club stamp on my right wrist and descend the steps ready to skank out, trigger fingering with *peng ting called Madisons* (I am familiar with the vernacular). The sound system's banging out a familiar tune that has everyone signing along. It's packed and the black boys don't like it if you push, it's game over if you step on their crisp, white footwear.

I've seen the pictures posted online: scantily-clad ravers

donning denim short shorts, or batty riders as they are called I believe, adorned with tattoo sleeves and nose piercings. Yes, I've seen the pictures of the posers with their rum and cokes, the couples, the just-met-on-the-dancefloors, the dry-humpers, the grinders, the lesbians, the Asians. All under one roof. Trap tune after trap tune. I swear, the only thing missing, I've heard others say, was the presence of hot hostesses – the ones that come to your table and give you the personal treatment to make you feel all special.

Gone now. Instead, I live with the pretence of being a public-school attending, classical music connoisseur. Rachmaninov. Come off it! Would struggle to spell it...

That's it.

I clamber forward. Clearly this man could be a problem. There is a funny stench and I don't like the whiff of it one bit. This could turn out worse than the Elephant and Castle roundabout debacle or Crossrail being delayed. I stand up ready to bulldoze my way towards the front of this little bus, but the young school boy with his baggy bottoms beats me to the aisle. He has the right idea, that great British fighting spirit, I'll be his back-up instead. I simply can't let this intruder with the rucksack hijack my campaign. Time to take back control.

DEAN

I get the shot in focus and squint my eyes to frame the image better, like what them proper photographers do at weddings, chemists and police stations. I'm in the perfect position. Even though it's sort of cloudy out, the light, at this moment, is just right. My back is bent forward to help me zoom in a bit more. I'm almost falling off my chair. My finger shakes with the pressure, ready to press down on the button and snap this scene. *Snap, snap, snap, snap, snap.* I take loads. *Snap, snap, snap, snap, snap.* And loads more just in case. Everyone hears me shooting, and starts looking at me funny like I'm crazy. I'm not crazy, Louis. This is art. It's not my fault I don't have an actual camera is it now?

I won't tell you what I captured, Louis; it wouldn't do it justice. All you need to know is if the papers got hold of them, boy, I would be a very rich man, you understand? It would make front page news. But they, and you, will have to wait till the book is published. *Hoxton Heroes* I'll call it and it'll be a picture book that'll sort of have a story to it too. It'll show how Hoxton has changed down the years, how it used to be rubbish and rundown, but now it's impossible to live around here for love nor money. It'll have my name on the front and will be available to buy from all good book shops, and online too. It'll be bought by them new-fangled hipsters from the bookshop in Brick Lane and there will be a gallery in Hoxton Square showing some of the shots from the book. When the gallery opens, people will sip their bottles of Stella slowly and talk with their hands. People will buy my work and little stickers will be put on the frame and I won't be homeless and dirty anymore. See, I have a plan to get out of this mess, Louis.

And after that, I will be well known in the area and across the whole of London. Maybe even the world, Louis. They will ask me to go into schools and give talks to the students about how I was once a bad egg with no future, who used to hang around with the wrong crowd, who overcame troubles with drink and drugs, but then managed to turn my life around because of my passion for photography. It will go really well. I will wear jeans that fit and smart brown shoes with the little tiny holes in them and they will invite me back the following year, and the year after that.

Right now though, I'm a builder without tools, a bus driver with no licence, a prossy without a pussy. I take picture after picture without an actual camera. I have nothing but these clothes on my back, my need for a bit of gear, and a girlfriend who could be locked up today. Karen's been my rock these past few months but she's due in court this morning, some old anti-social political crap, so she wants me there when she meets her new solicitor. He's new and young apparently, so she's nervous she might get locked up. If she gets sent down, I don't know what I'll do with myself.

I think I love her, Louis. She's kind to me. If I want something, she usually gets it for me. And she's not... what's the word? Maternal is it? No. Materialistic. She even gets angry if I get my hands on gifts to give her, beer or fags and stuff. She's living in a squat on the Holloway Road at the moment but unlike this bus, which is twisty and winding and long, we're tryna get back on the straight and narrow. We just need a push start, a helping hand, a friendly face to get us on our way again.

I'm struggling at the moment. I've spent the pony I got off Quick Quid on gear. Gear that's long gone. I went into one of them Somalian internet cafés at the back of Chapel Market the other day, 50p for a half hour, and applied on the website. On the form, I said I was a teacher and that my next payday was next week and they sent me the money in minutes. It was kinda too easy to be honest, Louis. I'm waiting on some money from the social but I should be able to pay them back on Friday 'cos I owe them money already. I really need to buy a real camera too so I don't know what I'm gonna do yet. I saw one I liked in Cash Converters and I told them to keep it for me; the lovely girl behind the counter said she would.

Snap, snap, snap, snap, snap.

Louis... I can't remember the last time I properly washed. Don't see the point. I only own dirty clothes and I don't need to impress nobody, I have a girlfriend now. After a while, you get used to the dirt under your nails and the bits in your beard and the bugs in your hair and the itch in your arse and the throbbing in your dick. When you're living on the streets, you have bigger fish to fry.

Snap, snap, snap, snap, snap.

I just really wish I had a proper camera to store all the memories. All the things I've seen down the years. I know every nook and cranny of Hoxton, I mean, I used to live there, and there, under there, behind that. All over this area, back when Hoxton was a proper shithole. Oh Louis, it used to get proper wild around here. But boy hasn't it half changed! I barely recognise it these days. There are these new buildings everywhere. Shops are different. The people have changed too. It's clear the council have forgotten about folk like us, Louis, and it breaks my heart. That's why I need the camera to belong again.

There's still so much to see though. Sometimes I just look out the window and smile and imagine if I had a bit of money, a job, a house, a car and a family how happy I could be here. Thing is though, round here, no money means no happiness.

And what's life without happiness? That's the reality for folk like me, the forgotten ones of this broken society. Don't get me wrong, Hoxton is an area with a lot of history: Hitchcock Studios, Fat Les, you know even the Krays were born here before moving down Bethnal Green. But nothing is how it used to be. No real identity anymore, Louis. These days, Hoxton is just a mish-mash of clothes, colours and cunts.

The roads are so small. The buses squeeze past each other like they want to give each other a hug and it's very nice of the woman to tell everyone what road we're on all the time. It must get pretty tiring though, I mean, her voice must get sore speaking to everyone all day. The black box where she lives looks like this wouldn't you say, Louis?

> **392 to Highbury Corner**
> **9:19 AM**

It's proper clean and shiny inside this bus like one of them fancy council bedsits they put you up in for a day, until a Romanian family move in with eight kids.

When you think about it, Louis, this bus is like a Wetherspoon's; it's a proper mix of people. Look around, you got businessmen in posh suits and pissheads in rags and cheeky kids, the rich, the poor, the black, the white, the sober, the drunk – all squashed in on this tiny little red bus. I turn round in my seat and take pictures of the schoolboy and the schoolgirl chatting away at the back, the football fan next to me, the half-caste girl who is pretty but angry-looking at the same time. I snap them all. Hang on... That's an idea. Maybe I should just focus on this bus journey in my book, Louis. The passengers who get on and everything I see looking out the window. I could call it *The Hoxton Bus Journey* or something, or maybe just *Journey*. I think I'm actually on to something. People and places, Louis. People and places.

Look at him here, Louis. Another of them new arty-farty students. One of them 'look-at-me-I-work-in-fashion' types. Is he 'avin' a laugh? In them poofter clothes, old man sandals with socks, long patterned dress thing like he's pretending to be Chinese when he's actually from Chelmsford. Hair shaved on the sides and long and wavy in the middle. Looks like he has make-up on too don't it, Louis? There's black shit around his eyes and shiny stuff around his mouth. More piercings than a cow. He looks like the old Dead or Alive Pete Burns mixed with the new *Celebrity Big Brother* Pete Burns, don't he, Louis? You know who I'm taking about don't ya'? The dead one. He stands there, listening to his music, while two podgy Indian women behind look at him appalled. It's the perfect pic. *Snap*. The shutter closes. Another one for the book. Just got in there before we drove off again.

There's a skill to this art, Louis. As an amateur photographer, it's about choices. A fat man with a teardrop tattoo or two in an England top eating a bagel isn't really a good picture. It probably wouldn't make the book, but a fat man with tattoos in an England top being stared at by a toddler in a pushchair does. I'm not an angles man; it's about the story for me. People and places.

Look, Louis, can you see him? I think I have an even better shot of the man at the front than the one I took earlier. You can't? Let me get those fingers ready. He looks like he might be lost or has shit his pants and doesn't want to sit down (might explain the bad smell). There is something not quite right and I think I know why... but I might need some help.

'Do you like football mate?' I ask the fella next to me.

'No,' he says, looking down then looking at me.

'Rugby?'

'No mate.'

'Cricket?'

'I'm not big on sports to be honest mate, I'm blind,' he says.

'Oh, right you are,' I say, then turn to focus my camera on the man at the front again and take another few photos. 'I bet that Muslim has a bomb in his bag ya' know?' I tells him, the man sat next to me. He looks like someone I want to help, we're both suffering in some way, I can see that even though he can't. I carry on snapping.

'What's that mate?' He asks, maybe his blindness has affected his hearing too.

'There's a bomb in there... I bet ya'.' I says, proud of myself, one eye still on the man with the bag as I continue to snap away, then, I try my luck. 'You got 40p, mate?' Like my late mother used to say, God rest her soul, if you don't ask, you don't get.

The blind man's face looks twisted and red and confused. His eyes look like two grey marbles through two tiny slits in his face. I take more pictures of the man at the front; my fingers work their magic. They'll all thank me for this later. I zoom in on something black in his hands, it's edge of the seat stuff. Something strange is happening now, look Louis. The blind man next to me with the white stick gets up slowly and walks towards the front of the bus and towards the man. Look, other people are getting involved too. You seeing this, Louis? You watching? It's like a Spoons at closing time, it's about to kick off. Thank your lucky stars I'm there to capture it all. *Snap, snap, snap...*

NATALIE

Could my life get any worse? I'm pregnant, pissed off and Boxer's at the back of this bus. I don't think he's seen me yet, but I've seen him, and I can hear him too, we all can. He's speaking so loudly on his phone, clearly trying to get those skanky schoolgirls' attention. Even though Boxer's nicer than his brother, this whole situation is messed up and I really don't need this stress right now. I can't be dealing with sharing this small space when the situation is so big.

I can hear what he's trying to do but it's all fake. Him speaking all 'street', like he's one of them wannabe roadmen, he's not really into that life. I know he's trying to play big man, giving it all that rudeboy talk, but I can see through all that. I've seen his cute baby pictures on the wall. I've seen him spill strawberry Mirinda down his school jumper. I know he wants to go uni and get a job in the City and get a girlfriend who he will marry. I know he wears his school tie done up properly, tucks his shirt in, says 'please' and 'thank you', lets old people on the bus first. He's considerate like that. He's not a rule-breaker, he's not his brother, he's just Boxer, a sweet sixteen-year-old.

I swear you catch so many smells sitting at the front of the bus. Honestly, you get whiffs of people with real bad BO when they get on and walk past. Some passengers look proper dirty too like they've been sleeping rough in Hackney City Farm all night or something. I try not to, but sometimes I make it obvious that someone smells because I screw up my face and spray some of that cheap perfume I got down Hoxton Market all around me. I always keep it in my bag because in my condition I can't take any risks catching anything. Thank God most bad smells aren't contagious like curry smells though, you know what they say, once you get curry smell stuck on your clothes, it never comes off. Ask any Indian.

The crackhead sitting on the other side smells so bad like he ain't washed for years, he's clearly got mental health problems too because he's on his knees pretending he's taking pictures and talking to himself, he hasn't even got a camera. I try not to look in case he flips and does something crazy but I kinda can't help myself having a little peek out the corner of my eye. He looks proper homeless, like one of them men that sleep in shop doorways with only a dirty sleeping bag and their woolly hat to keep them warm. It's sad really. He's making the sound effects with his mouth too, like children do when they're playing with an old camera that has no battery but pretend to take pictures anyway. I just don't get people like that. Weren't they brought up properly or something? Why do they have to stink so much as well? Why aren't they in some hospital or centre where trained people can look after them?

It's my own fault though I suppose, I dunno, I just felt like sitting near the front today, behind them priority seats. I wanted to sit somewhere where I could watch the world pass me by and forget about all the drama in my life. Sometimes I like looking out the window and pretending I'm all the different people: the business women in expensive-looking suits and loafers with the tassels, and posh people with Michael Kors handbags and fancy beige coats writing important emails on their phone, emails that use proper spelling and all the right grammar because they need to come across all professional if they want the business deal to go through. They probably have a 'Linking' profile which tells people where they work and what uni they went to – my girl Bethany was telling me this the other day, it's like Facebook but for posh people.

We cross Balls Pond Road; it finally feels like we're getting somewhere at last. There's a bit of white fluff from someone's jacket floating around the front of the bus like a bird that doesn't know where it wants to land, like it doesn't know where it should settle. It's soft but spikey at the same time. I hate them because sometimes they stick to you in the most random places and it's only when you go to the toilet or put make-up on in the mirror or something that you clock that it's probably just been cotching in your hair all day.

It's really raining now. Typical England, one minute it's fine and there's even a bit of sun to get excited about and then all of a sudden it turns mad and it starts to piss it down, proper hard too. It's like British weather is bi-polar like Stacey's mum from *Eastenders*. It's coming down and sticking to the windows like spider webs. There are tiny droplets clinging on like they are so desperate to get inside but they're not allowed because they doesn't have a contactless and the bus driver's acting proper harsh.

There's still a man standing up at the front, right by the driver. You always get a least one weirdo on a bus in London, but two today, on a bus this small, that's taking liberties. This one looks like a Muslim maybe. From Afghanistan or one of them countries there. One of them Asians that sells them Lycra Mobile phonecards and works long nights in Londis. Or maybe from Pakistan or Syria or one of them Indian countries. He's not even turning around, just standing there like he's the captain of a big ship watching the world go by. He has a bag over one of his shoulders like he could be about to get off at the next stop, but whenever the doors open, he just stands still. He doesn't move; he's like a statue in his green jacket and his black bag. He's acting all weird like he's trying to chirpse the driver – I know these Muslim men are allowed bare wives. And he's wearing this No Fear rucksack and dead Airwalk trainers like the ones you can get in Sports Direct. It's England's fault for letting all these Eastern European Muslim people in.

I hear Boxer still, speaking loudly at the back. Don't get it twisted, people only call him Boxer 'cos his initials are KO, he can't fight for shit. All boys his age have street names, his one sounds aggressive but trust me, he's not like that at all. His government name is Kehine Olupade. The only trouble he got into in school was for pointing out a mistake his Maths teacher made and he got sent out 'cos she was embarrassed. That's the story his brother told me anyway.

This is turning into one mad bus journey, one I'm not really feeling. I just want to get to Highbury already. I want to get to the hospital and get all this over and done with. I want to hear the baby's heartbeat and see its little body on the little screen. I want to make something of this mess without any more fuss and no more drama. I wanna get off this bus quickly and get back on track, get on the 271 and go to college in the evenings, and get my Level 3, start my own nursery (there's money in childcare, trust me). I wanna finish this book I'm writing 'cos this shit matters. This life I live is an important message for everybody. I'm gonna get Bethany to print it off for me when I'm done because she's a teaching assistant at Thomas Fairchild and she says they have a big photocopier in the staff room. I'll send it to Waterstones using a first-class stamp, so it gets there quickly. We could have the launch at Hoxton Hall. It might even be in the shops before Christmas.

It's got a bit intense all of a sudden. The fluff is still floating around, flirting with everybody, from person to person. The crackhead is talking loudly and still taking fake pictures with his dirty fingers, clicking away like he's in a nightclub or something. The film crew are struggling to get set up and these interviews they're planning are probably never gonna actually happen. The bus driver is speeding over humps too fast making everyone wobble about like one of them nodding toy dogs people used to have in the backs of their cars. The blind man with the football top is still bumping into people and banging his stick on every pole, I thought he was gonna be some hero but I think he was just moving away from the stinky tramp on the other side. The old lady looks nervous, gripping her shopping trolley so tight her hands look like they're turning proper red. There's still a man, all quiet and weird, standing there at the very front, not even moving really, just holding something small and black with his right hand and holding the pole in front of him with his left.

Those girls at the back still think they're bad, I can hear them chatting, trying to wind me up but I can't get myself too stressed, it's not good for the baby but they best know not to mess with me, I know people. I'm Hoxton to the core, like the Iceland or the Market or the man with the gammy teeth who sells carpets or the weirdo who works in the broken fridge shop and is always rolling his neck. Hoxton runs through my blood, out of my heart and round the body. If you shank me,

The 392

I bleed Hoxton, you understand? Those girls better watch themselves, even in my condition.

Life hasn't always been all honky-dory, all sweet and niceness, all Rosy and Jim. No way. I've been living in Hoxton since the days it was proper ghetts and getting yourself involved in the wrong crowd could get you killed. I've been living in Hoxton since before these little school girls could even walk, back when Hoxton Gardens was Burbage and long before Whitmore Primary was Shoreditch Park. I know my area like the back of hand. They should call me Queen of Hoxton, not that hipster place by Liverpool Street.

This bus is still going all round the ends like it's lost or something, or like it's one of them rival opps slipping in a new area and not wanting to be in one place for too long in case it gets spotted, shanked up and killed just for being in the wrong place at the wrong time. It's lucky I'm in no rush, my appointment is at ten thirty, which gives me enough time to decide what I'm gonna do about these little girls that think they can run up their mouth. Bet they're getting off at that sket school in Highbury.

The ends keep changing. There was once the proper tiny bus that used to go down Pitfield Street back in the day, it was proper tiny, even smaller than this. People got bare excited about it because they could go to Angel and go Woolworths or Sainsbury's if they were feeling posher than Iceland for a change. It was proper small though, it looked like a blue transit van that Amazon deliver parcels in and tailgate vulnerable granny drivers on the road. I used to get that little blue bus to Angel back in the day when you had to go to this one special shop down Chapel Market to get your school uniform, and after go Woolworths to get pick-n-mix and a *Best of Will Smith* CD that had a £3 sticker on it. Back then, when I had school, I used to have Rio fizzy drinks and chocolate Gold bars for breakfast and Walkers prawn cocktail crisps and Coke for lunch. Then I used to down a bottle of Fanta, fruit twist flavour to get one of my five-a-day, and be all hyper for Geography. All our diets used to be mad shit them times because we didn't know any better, so it was prawn cocktail crisps and Coke for lunch, and chicken and chips for dinner. Always chicken and chips for dinner.

Hoxton used to be mad rough though. People talk about Brixton, Peckham and Croydon but always forget about Hoxton, London Fields and Homerton. It was never easy living in the ends; it used to be mad. Mad mad. It wasn't all Vindaloo round here, trust me. There are a million stories I could write down about how hard life was for people like me. It's all important, from Britannia Leisure Centre to the job centre at the bottom of the market. All of it makes my story come alive because setting is important.

I mean Dad's Barbershop was a mad one altogether; that was the real Hoxton. It was a proper family run community shop, like an episode of *Desmond's*. It's where all the boys used to go to get a fresh trim to make sure they looked good for the girls like us. I went in a few times myself. I used to sometimes shave the sides of my hair, because when I was in school, I always liked looking different. The old man in there with grey high-top hair was the owner. Black barbers are always entertaining, they can take so long just to give you a little trim because halfway through they decide to get some food, usually a little jerk chicken with rice and peas and steamed veg from Belly's.

This bus is moving bare wild like the driver's a boy racer with a provisional licence from the estate or something, like one of them youts on stolen mopeds. She's whipping round the corners of Newington Green like it's shook or something so needs to get out the block quickly. These likkle schoolgirls who think they're big are starting to proper piss me off. They don't know who they're fucking with, trust me, my babyfather isn't a good man. One of them is chatting to Boxer and I bet they think they're winding me up, but they aren't, not really, they don't know my struggle. The life I've lived. They're nothing to me; I've fought some proper battles in my life.

As the bus leaves Dalston I move on to my second note of writing. Chapter two of nineteen maybe. I've got bare to say. All them bad stories growing in the days when people used to be embarrassed to say they lived in Hackney. This book could be one long movie like *Titanic* or *Gone With the Wind* or a whole series on Netflix. I've been living on the breadline years before

Hoxton and Dalston were full of hipsters in skinny jeans and pointy Chelsea boots.

The bus stops at the lights and starts humming like it's thinking long and hard about how life used to be, like I like to do sometimes. If I could go back, how I would have made different decisions. Chosen different people. All of a sudden the bus speeds up fast again. People are jiggling about and looking at the driver like she doesn't know how to drive properly but I'm used to people driving fast. My mum once had a boyfriend who used to drive a Chrysler. I remember this time we were coming back from my nan's, think it must have been Christmas; she lives in Hornchurch and it usually took forty minutes through Bow and that on the A13. I remember this time, we did it in twenty, I know because I had my new Baby G watch on. We were weaving between cars like it was Formula One and he was Michael Schwarzenegger. I was never scared though, most of the time, even though it was pretty mad still how we somehow made it home in one piece.

The trampy photographer is on his knees now. We're not even far from Highbury Corner and the bus is packed still. Everyone's facing the front and holding on tight like we're on a Ryanair flight about to land on the runway. People are not even listening to their music or really paying attention to what's happening outside, you can tell by their faces. They're all stiff and tense. They're all just facing the front like it's a cinema and the film showing is *Saw* or something. Something mad scary.

The blind man in the football top looks completely fed up. The old lady looks nervous. The rain is falling hard now and the streets around Canonbury look kinda shiny but dirty at the same time. It's the type of weather that causes headaches, one of them tension ones. It's grey and it feels like the inside of your brains are all squashed together. I sit sort of half-turned, half looking ahead, half looking at Boxer who is still chatting to the schoolgirls at the back. I'm feeling a little bit lonely all of a sudden.

Then, as the bus gets faster, I see him coming down the bus, from the corner of my eye; I don't know whether to turn away and pretend I haven't seen or try to chat to him. Then, I make a quick decision, I lunge forward to touch him and end up tugging him and grabbing his school blazer in a kinda rough way because the bus is driving all bumpy.

'Boxer,' I say. I might as well be the bigger person, being pregnant and that. 'Thought it was you... what's good?' I ask. He looks young and surprised and sweet and kinda sexy all rolled into one.

'Good, well, not bad... you?'

He doesn't look that surprised to see me. He must have clocked me already from the back. 'Yeah same, just a bit,' I look down at my belly, 'pregnant.'

There's not much he can say to that. He knows the story

and he knows what his brother's like. It's raining proper hard now but the tiny bit of light from the window is shining on his face and afro. He's letting his hair grow out and already it suits him. He smiles a shy smile and licks his lips like boys who think they're buff do. He is cute though, there's no doubt about it.

'I feel bad about all this. My brother is acting kinda deep.' Boxer's words are slow and serious like he actually means it, like he wouldn't have treated me this way if the slider was on the other sock. He looks me in the eyes, then down towards my breasts and then nervously down at his Kickers. I don't see his brother in him; Boxer's too kind for that. The bus is getting bumpier and people are swaying all around us but we are still. His phone starts ringing in his pocket and I can tell by his face that he doesn't want to answer it, but he takes a deep breath and does.

'*Hey... 'sup?*' he says, his face has dropped, he looks scared. '*It's not a good time to talk... I'm on the bus innit... What, now?*' He pauses for a long moment – his face looks all pale and stressed all of a sudden. '*What are you planning to do?*' Another long pause. He's biting the skin of his bottom lip and staring into the distance. The person on the other side has obviously put the phone down. His face looks so worried as he puts his phone back in his pocket. I don't ask him who it was.

'Let me sit here for a bit... before I fall.'

I move my bag off the seat next to me and he pulls up his

school trousers before he sits down. I wish I could hug him or rest my head on his shoulder like they do in the movies but you never know who's watching. There's always someone watching in the ends. The rain is falling heavy and Boxer is there looking at me and I'm looking at him. None of us say anything for a while, just stare. The mood on the bus is still mad tense but sitting next to Boxer I'm starting to feel better. He puts his hand on my thigh and says, 'Family matters,' like he's a mature thirty-year-old and then I get this weird tingly feeling all over my body and things just start to feel all funny inside. And I start to think that maybe it's time to put my phone away and start a new chapter for real.

The man's still at the front and the atmosphere is making everyone feel uncomfortable, it's getting all dramatic like at the end of *Cool Runnings* when the bobsleigh is about to crash. Then, as the bus slows and stops past a pub by a Sainsbury's Local, something strange happens. The man with the bag at the front turns round a little – he looks scared and weak like a baby red nose pitbull who's not learned to be naughty and stubborn yet. He has a blank look on his face and it's starting to feel like a scene from *Luther* or something and I swear I feel the baby kick.

RAY

A terrorist! A bloody fucking terrorist on this bus, on its first day of fucking service too. What a fucking surprise, you couldn't make it up! This country's gone to pot: niggers running riot in Tottenham, kids on mopeds stealing mobiles off mums, and Muslims making bombs in bedrooms to blow up buses. I'm about to die and what will the police do? Fuck all that's what. We're *all* about to fucking die and the state are just gonna sit back in their fancy chairs down in Westminster and let 'em. No guesses either what this rag probably looks like, even for a blind git like me I bet I wouldn't be far off. He's probably a bloody United fan too.

I would like to say it's been fun, I suppose, back in the day it was for a time. But life now is shit to be honest, not like it used to be, so maybe I shouldn't be so angry, maybe this is my time to go, maybe this fucking knobhead blowing us all up is a blessing in disguise. I should have really gone on that day in Cardiff to be frank. I just hope I have my sight back in my next life so I can see my kids again and my beloved Millwall. Watch action at The Den from up there in the clouds. Maybe it won't be so bad.

I sat down again. Had to. This lion isn't as brave as he thought (or once fought), the drink and drugs have messed with my head, the balances are all wrong, I mean what was I thinking? I can't do nothing now look at me. What could I really do? I'm finished. I'm no hero; I can't see shit. To be honest, I'm just glad to have got away from the pissing crackhead prodding me with his crackhead fingers, couldn't take the stench anymore. I felt my way to a new seat on the other side and found a new place to sit. It was a good move. Whoever I'm sat next to now smells decent, clean, Nivea shower gel, Paco Rabanne eau du toilette, probably a banker. Or lawyer. Nice office, work email, burgundy loafers, colourful socks. Used to have a lot of those when I had my cab. Can smell them a mile off, used to see them coming too. But this fella here next to me is fidgeting all over the gaff, unzipping pockets, opening and closing the clasp of his bag and shaking papers about nervously it sounds like. He's probably as worried as I am, as we all are, about this fella up front. It's tense like we're on the brink of relegation and we all know a parachute payment won't help a promotion push. Everyone has gone quiet. You can just about hear the heavy breathing of all the passengers. Even the schoolkids at the back just whisper now. Only the crackhead is making a sound, snapping away and making clicking noises with his mouth like he's a camera.

I suppose I could just get off and walk the rest of the way but no one else is it seems. Well, at least I haven't heard anybody get off yet. And if I did get off, then what? I'll just be feeling my way round Canonbury whacking my white stick hoping I somehow end up at the GPs in time for my nine forty-five appointment. Fuck that! Why should I let this brown fucker win? This is my country, my north London, my city. That's where this country has gone wrong, too soft. I'll stay on till the bitter end and whatever happens I can die happy knowing I've made my country proud. *Two World Wars, one World Cup.*

You won't believe it but I used to look the bollocks, trust me. Much slimmer than this beer gut suggests, I'm telling you. I used to get all the girls from here to Walthamstow; I didn't even give a fuck if they had a fella already. A real fucking wide-boy Casanova I was. I used to feel irresistible by the end of my second pint. That's what London life was like back then, proper rough. Not like now. Just real men having a pint or ten and having a punch-up, no knives, no guns, definitely no bloody bombs, just fists. And we were always careful of the face of course; we all had work in the morning. Who would want to go out with me now? I'm a burden, can't even look after myself properly, can't 'look' at anything any bloody more.

Feels like Dalston now. The traffic is heavy and outside is noisier. I remember Dalston a few years back, proper no-go zone it was. Wouldn't find me dead round here with my cab, tell you that for free. Dead cert runners if they wanted a drop off at Dalston, or anywhere in Hackney to be honest. Runs to Homerton, Hackney Wick, Clapton, no way, wouldn't see a penny.

I've been back to The Den only once since becoming a blind bastard. Not an occasion to remember, a terrible FA Cup replay against Dagenham and Redbridge back in... oh, 2011, it must have been. I didn't really fancy it to be honest, I knew it wouldn't be the same and it doesn't live long in the memory. Hearing Hendo score a hat-trick isn't quite the same as seeing the ball hit the back of the net three times. I thought maybe a punch-up before kick-off might spice things up a bit – there was talk of some of the West Ham lot showing to make things a bit tasty, but they obviously didn't want it and steered clear. We smashed them 5-0 in the end, a young Harry Kane scored a couple I remember, he's pretty good these days ain't he? I haven't bothered going back after that; it just ain't the same anymore.

But I tell ya' what though, England away was something else. Always bound to come back with a few broken bones and tasty bruises. There were always a few fuckers who took it too far but generally it was always good harmless fun. Boozing it with our guts out, getting more pissed in the sun by the second. By six, we're chucking plastic chairs in the main square, pissing off the police, pissing on the street and stumbling in through the turnstiles to cheer on the boys. Those were the good old days. We'd sing songs till our throats were sore, win, lose or draw, head straight to the bar and get straight back on the beers chanting *Rule Britannia, Britannia rules the waves.*

What's going on? This driver is taking all of us for a ride that's for sure. I'm feeling every bump, every twist and turn, feels like I'm on a fucking ride in Thorpe Park. It's like the driver has a plan to drive badly to make the bastard bomber get off, but it's clearly not working. In my time, I've seen some bad driving of course but this feels like something else altogether. Incompetence won't kill a terrorist, I can tell ya' that now.

In Cardiff, I clearly remember one particular black Manc that day I lost my sight. This big gorilla bastard with fucking huge black biceps punching, kicking and stamping on me over and over. I was his human punch bag. I tried grabbing his foot, but the others just ploughed in. Head, ribs, balls, they got me everywhere. They even grabbed me round my neck and pounded my head into the concrete. Savage bastards. Nike ticks, Vodafone letters and Red Devil logos in and out of vision. Don't get me wrong, the others were getting stuck in too but this big Django-looking nigger had it in for me and I couldn't tell ya' why. He was a right fucking unit. They only stopped when a couple of the lads came down the road and saw what was going on. That's when the cunts ran away. The lads thought I was dead when they found me, that's what they said. As I said before, I wish I was.

The geezer next to me is still acting all nervous. I can feel it. He's shifting about and wiggling uneasily, fiddling with his bag still, picking it up and putting it down again. He knows there's something fishy going on with this fella at the front. The driver speeds on, bouncing over the speed bumps and then around Newington Green, I think, when the geezer's phone rings.

'*Karen, yes, it's Levi.*'

My stomach knots itself up all of a sudden at the sound of his voice and that pain in the pit of my gut gets worse.

'*Are you there already?*' he asks. He's clearly well-spoken but something ain't right. There's a bit of a pause and my stomach is killing. '*I'm on the bus. I should be there in ten, fifteen minutes.*'

Levi? Levi? That ain't no English name. John, Graham, Peter... Ray, now these are real English names. Real Anglo-Saxon history, strong men, brave men, great men. Levi? Sounds like a make of denim jeans to me, sounds like a black. The man's a fucking nigger, I can hear it in his voice now, one of them third generation Jamaicans. History of crime: GBH, domestic violence, that sort of stuff, I met his kind before, they're no good for the country except for increasing the crime figures and sprouting half-breed sprogs, this ain't the 1950s. Lady luck's just not smiling down on me today, first I sit next to a stinking crackhead who tries to make me his best mate, then I sit next a nigger, and to top it all off, the icing on the bloody cake, there's still a bloody

Muslim with a bomb in his bag. Someone up there is taking the fucking Michael.

'*Are you there already?*' he asks the person on the other end again. The reception must be bad. It's clear what sort of geezer this is, one of those that don't even know the words to *God Save the Queen*, but happy to sponge off our benefits and use our schools and hospitals. One of those traitors that says he supports Barcelona instead of his local team. Would rather order a Captain Morgan's and Coke than a proper pint. Sells weed on the side and has one of them cannabis farms in his bedroom using electricity he doesn't even pay for. Goes to the gym three times a day to look big on a night out and pull a white girlfriend. Cheats on his white girlfriend. This country's full of them. Niggers who think they run the world but the first to complain when the police rightly stop and search them.

'*OK well, don't worry, as I said, I'm on my way, I should be there in ten, fifteen minutes,*' he says smugly, like a right old sly fucking cunt.

I've said it already and I'll say it again; this country's gone to pot.

We speed on. I hear heavy rain, the wipers swishing hard left to right, the indicators blinking and hearts beating. But how much longer? In the movies, they say when you're about to die, your whole life flashes before your eyes, but this flash is long and blinding. The bus is going faster now, apart from the sound of the splashing puddles outside, it's all gone quiet, even the crackhead has stopped snapping. I can't see him but I can tell just the presence of the man at the front is making everyone nervous. It's not because they are on their way to work or school and they don't want to go. It's worse than that; I can feel it. I can smell, taste, hear and feel everyone's fear.

That nigger Levi here is off the phone now, so against my better judgement, I strike up a little conversation, size up the cunt. It's all fucked anyway, I realise that now.

'You scared sunshine?' I say to him coldly.

'Nah, I'm good mate, you?' he says.

Yes, inside I'm shitting my pants. Black or white or even Muslim we're all going to die, together as one. We both sit silent.

'Think you'll do it this year?' he asks suddenly.

'Do what mate?' I ask flatly, everyone wants to talk to old Ray today.

'Play-offs. My old man's a Millwall fan actually.'

LEVI

I remember the colour so clearly; I had never seen anything like it. A bright golden orange like the lava from a volcano. It was in fact an eruption of light. Even though it was dark and pretty late, the flames were so blindingly bright I could've worn sunglasses. The flames felt so hot too, I could feel it pricking my skin but I still just wanted to stay and watch the power of the flames at work. I remember watching as the fire engulfed the interior: the seats, the poles, the steering wheel, the windows, the stairs, both the lower deck and upper deck all aflame. After a short while, my eyes started stinging from the smoke billowing out but I stood there still, as the ash flew about everywhere like hot summer snowflakes and tears streamed from my eyes. I never thought I would see a sight like this, a fire causing so much damage, a bus dying in this way.

All along Tottenham High Road, complete chaos, like something from the news when you hear about Syria and

Afghanistan. Buildings on fire and hooded kids egging the police on, swearing and cussing, hurling rocks and glass bottles and messaging people from all over London who got the call to get involved. Police horses charging into crowds of people, crowds that included little kids, and behind the horses, an army of police officers in riot gear. Batons, shields and swear words. It was madness. I could see why people were angry. I was angry. And to top it all off, we had police officers not even from the area, not even from London some of them, tryna' tell *us* what to do and how to feel. It got everyone ever madder. This was Tiverton, Tottenham, not Hull.

As the night carried on, the troubles got worse. I remember the broken glass showering down on us like rain. And the plumes of smoke from the bus on fire still cascading into the sky and clouding the whole of Tottenham, and the whole of north London, basically. Police vans barricading and blocking off certain roads. But it didn't stop us. We ran around aimlessly like it was one big game, one big playground. People jumped on abandoned police cars, climbed over garden fences and smashed shop windows. We felt all emotions: anger and ecstasy, joy and pain. We were hurt and wanted to cause as much damage as possible, get back at the police, get back at David Cameron and the Tory government and get back at the racist systems and this was the only voice we had. Forget marches in Westminster Square, this was our own special form of protest, in the comfort of our own area.

Like this little bus journey, it's been bumpy at times, but I've turned a few corners since the court case in 2011. I had to do my time, clear my name and move forward quickly, and trust me, that wasn't easy. Wearing hi-viz on the high street, sweeping roads and loading bin bags into the back of vans while my boys from the ends watched from across the road, laughing and cussing. That shit was tough. But I studied hard in the evenings; St. Ann's Library became my second home. Ever since primary people have always told me I was good at arguing, something that comes from my days at secondary school, arguing with everyone that Man United were better than Arsenal, comparing Keane with Viera, Giggs with Pires, Scholes with Fabregas. To be fair, no one could compare with Henry though, that guy was class. Even though we were about five minutes from White Hart Lane, no one rated Tottenham; they've always been shit.

I was destined to work in law from young, and it was more than just because for black parents it's one of only three desired career paths – the others being doctor or engineer of course – but being a lawyer always seemed to be a career that played to my skills, debating, fighting injustice, going blow to blow with the po-po.

2011 was a setback to say the least. I can't lie; I got sucked in by all the Mark Duggan, 'hard stop' stuff. It mattered to me, he mattered to me, I knew him. Not personally, but everyone in the ends knew *of* him, saw him about the estate from time to time in his Benz. He was like what Escobar was to Medellin in *Narcos*. He was one of those faces of the area, god-like in many ways, not just him, but his whole family too. It was all the *Mark had a gun* talk that got us really angry in the days after he was shot dead by people paid to protect the community. If he had a gun, he ain't gonna shoot it at police officers now was he? As I said to the magistrates that day, this isn't America. I had to do something, I needed to make a difference, defend the defenceless. That's why I became a solicitor, fight injustice, one case at a time. But, after that day at Highbury Corner Magistrates, I had to clear my name. First, I got myself an office assistant job at a little law firm in Angel. White Lion Street. I say job, but it felt like doing work experience again. I was doing the small stuff: filing, archiving, running to the Pret on the corner to get everyone lattes and fancy crayfish salads. They didn't even ask about my past when they unofficially 'employed' me, just paid me £100 a week from the petty cash till and wrote me a pretty good reference at the end of it too. I didn't have a suit, not really, I just had some trousers I used to wear for school – they came up short around the ankles, 'waiting for a flood' my mum used to say – a shirt I got from Primark that was too big around the neck and a tie that was hideous: stripy and fat. I looked ridiculous but it didn't matter, I was given a tiny taste of the life I wanted to live. Slowly, I was beginning to redeem myself; even Mum was becoming proud of me again.

I used some of the money I earned to get little bits of shopping for the house now and then, milk and bread and things. She appreciated that.

Feeling inspired after this, I blagged my way into a decent college in west London to do a few A-Levels and a BTEC. The best part was that I could do A-Level Law as an enrichment lesson on Wednesdays and this felt like a blessing to me. Got an 'A' in it of course. The teachers were amazing I must say, gave me every chance to do well, recognised my desire and helped me get the grades to get to university. I remember all their names. I have to say teachers don't get the credit they deserve, man, some of them were miracle workers I swear.

I was happy to go anywhere for uni to be honest: London Met, Roehampton, University of East London, somewhere close-ish, but the careers advisor at sixth form said I was aiming too low and I should try a 'red brick' or a 'Russell Group'. I didn't even know what she was talking about or who Russell was. I didn't care about the reputation of the uni; I wanted the qualification so I could start earning. I've always been confident of impressing people in interviews; I'm personable, well-spoken (sometimes), driven and ambitious, my CV says, so that never worried me. I needed a Law degree to get things going. As advised by my teachers, I ended up at the University of Sussex in Brighton. The furthest south I had been before this was Croydon. It was a good choice in the end, it was far enough to feel like I was getting a genuine university experience away from the daily grind of London life and still close enough to get back to N17 in a couple of hours, see Mum, do laundry and play Sunday league.

The uni thing was weird at first, I can't lie, it was hard for me to fit in for ages. There were only a handful of black people on my course; it took some getting used to. I stood out in the lecture theatre; they all had come from private schools and were more worldly than I was at the time. Seminars were daunting too, the tutor would ask me questions and sometimes I just couldn't get the words out. But I didn't let that bother me; I worked hard, most of the time, and always got the essays in. Slowly, my confidence was growing. The years flew by and, despite a shaky start, I finished with a 2:1. More than that though, I finally felt confident talking to people, articulating my point, elaborating my views on topical matters: politics, the monarchy, rising interest rates.

The day my result was confirmed, I went down to the seafront and watched the tide come in as the sun came up. It was like the sea was breathing and I was breathing freely with it for the first time in my life. I sat there, freezing cold but buzzing. It was only during my graduation when I walked up to the stage, spudded Sanjeev Baskhar in front of my family and a few of my boys from home, did the feeling of pride hit me – I had redeemed myself. In my hands, at last, I was clutching the paper which meant I had a certified Law degree. And the days of messing about on Tottenham High Street, eating chicken and chips with our hoods up, and the London Riots seemed like a distant nightmare. Now I was not just the first in my family to go to university but I had an actual degree. Trust, redemption was sweet.

I'm engaged to a girl I met at Sussex now. A real *Made in Chelsea* type, grew up in Barnes, went to boarding school somewhere out in the country, has a posh voice – 'well-spoken' she calls it – but has the ability to mix it up depending on the crowd and context, and a dad who made his money in the City. Before her, I had never gone out with a white girl, but I knew from the first time I saw her in that Brighton seafront nightclub, she was the one for me. It was Halloween I remember, I was the *Fresh Prince of Bel-Air*, she was *Sabrina the Teenage Witch* and in the world of nineties popular culture, it was meant to be. I hatched a plan. I went over to the DJ booth and requested a particular song, he agreed once I told him why. I bought two Malibu and Cokes and bowled over to her and as the track began to play, I started reciting the *Fresh Prince* theme tune, the extended version, word for word. I even did all the actions. It worked a treat, as she sipped on her free drink and I thought *if anything this cab is rare, but I thought no forget it*, we swapped numbers. Hard to believe how quick things have moved. We secured a small flat in Manor House last week. Life is much better now, but this just feels like the start, I have business cards and a silver business card holder, I have a client list and a badge with my face on and a lanyard with the firm's logo. Little things, but now I wake up and finally feel fulfilled.

I didn't steal the bag of basmati from Tesco. Of course I didn't. Like everybody in the area, I was angry and frustrated with the police after what happened to Mark in Tottenham Hale, but I didn't loot a single thing that night. I'm too proud of my area to help destroy it. I posted the picture online as a joke and things got out of hand. The reaction was unbelievable. I'm not even sure how they found me in the end, but one morning, literally as I was making toast, I had feds banging at my door. Mum was fuming. Shouting at the police officers saying there must have been some mistake and they've got the wrong person. 'Not my boy! Not my boy!' she shouted over and over. 'Get your dirty racist hands off him!' The next day I was taken to court, and well, you know the rest. It blew up. I was in every paper in the country. OK, so my face was partially covered but it was clearly me, the nose, the eyes, the clothes, the gloves. The evidence was there for the whole nation to see. The picture was everywhere, in every newspaper in the country.

Today is another milestone on that journey from shame. My first case this morning involves a well-known local: Ms. Karen Miller, 39, of no fixed abode. The criminal history of a conventional 'crackhead' – hate that word – theft, aggravated burglary, Class A drug possession, that sort of stuff, spanning years. Today she's being trialled for another minor offence, but today, as it's my first case, it's a rather big deal to me. I'm sufficiently suited: waistcoat and loafers. I've even had a fresh shape-up. I looked over the case notes, many times and I know how I'm going to play it. I feel sufficiently prepared. My mentor should be there too, an opportunity to impress.

Some people have got off here and there but the man with the bag is still at the front, and so is this strange feeling that something isn't quite right with him. He has a rucksack on his back and has a big beard and what with everything that's been going on recently, I can tell everyone is on edge. I'm not much of a reader, and in my line of work I shouldn't judge books by covers but he *is* acting strange. At the beginning, I assumed he must be getting off soon and that's why he was standing there but his bag looks bulky and cumbersome. Surely not though? Those are old tactics. If a terrorist wants to make a point, don't they hire white vans and plough into people outside busy train stations or catch those walking to work on some bridge? Should I phone the police? What would I say? There's a man at the front of a bus minding his own business with a bag on his back. That's every Londoner on a Monday morning. How ridiculous, it's probably nothing. I saw a sign that said: *reporting something unusual won't hurt you*. It's probably nothing.

My phone rings, it's Karen.

'*Karen, yes, it's Levi... are you there already?*' I ask. Silence and then a sizzling on the line. Her voice isn't coming through clear but I press on. *'I'm on the bus, I should be there in ten, fifteen minutes.'*

The crackhead is taking a flurry of fake pictures.

'Are you there already?' I ask her again, louder this time. She sounds out of it even at this time of the morning.

Her response is wordy and slurred. For a person with previous and a regular through the court system, this is going to be a tricky one, she doesn't sound completely well.

'OK well, don't worry, as I said, I'm on my way, I should be there in ten, fifteen minutes.'

The phone is cut dead before I get out the last words, something wrong at her end.

As I put my phone back in my pocket, I see that the man at the front has something in his hands and I start to worry. I don't want to die today, I can't. I don't want all my hard work to be undone with the pressing of a single button. I don't want to be blown to bits. There's still so much I want to do with my life, still so much to achieve: get promoted at work, become a partner, get married, have children and a nice detached four-bed house in Farncombe. I want to grow old with Liv, go on trips to the theatre and nice holidays to Las Vegas and the Amalfi Coast and Buenos Aires and take endless photos to store on the cloud. She's the one, she must be. I love how she carries herself with such grace through the daily madness of London life. I love the way she moves through a crowd. I love her strawberry blonde hair, her fringe and her quirky fashion sense. I like how she wears that tight leather skirt and the peep-toe black boots when she's meeting my friends and wants to make that extra effort. I love how smart she is and how witty she can be. She's perfect for me. Even my family love her (and I'm sure they'll rather I'd marry a black girl).

I have an idea. I'm going to do it tonight, book a table at a nice restaurant in the City and do something brave. I'm going to do what none of my boys back in Totty have done yet. I'm going to propose to her. It feels like the perfect time to settle down properly, keep the momentum going. Get married. It makes sense. We'll do it at Woodberry Wetlands in the summer after next. The ceremony will be held in a marquee overlooked by the tower blocks, it'll be a millennial wedding, her rich family and my colourful one interwoven. My nan will have her doubts about our choice of venue, she'll want something more traditional but she'll be pleasantly surprised to see it all come together. The reception will be a short walk around the reservoir by the old Coal House. Perfect picture opportunities. Dinner and speeches. There'll be a free bar of course. I can just imagine the faces of my family when they stroll up to the counter and realise they won't have to pay for any of their double Wray & Nephews, straight. There'll be the best music too, a homage to my West Indian roots: John Holt – *Stick By Me*. Morgan Heritage – *Down By The River*. Beres Hammond – *They Gonna Talk*. Luther Vandross – *Never Too Much*. Krosfyah – *Pump Me Up*. Jagged Edge – *Let's Get Married*.

Ken Boothe – *Everything I Own*. Janet Kay – *Silly Games*. Buju Banton – *One to One*. Desmond Dekker – *Pickney Gal*. Before midnight everyone's on their feet doing the Candy slide. We'll make a professional wedding video of the day too and we'll post it on YouTube a few months after so all our friends and family can revisit our special day. I'm going to do it tonight. I'm going to propose. Today is the beginning of the rest of my new life...

I'm nudged on the shoulder.

'You scared sunshine?' the football fan with the white stick says, his voice gravelly and thuggish.

'Nah, I'm good mate, you?' I say.

After a longish pause and studying his old Millwall top, I ask, 'Think you'll do it this year?'

'Do what mate?' he retorts defensively.

'Play-offs. My old man's a Millwall fan actually.'

He breaks into a half smile.

GLORIA

I've decided. I'm staying on to Highbury. It's my only option if I want to see my Al again. All I want to do is hug him and kiss him and rub his bad knees better (and he can kiss mine). I want to feel his strong touch again. I want to feel welcome, loved, alive. I want to be dead, dear.

There used to be a bus garage around here, I'm sure of it. Right there behind the fire station. I remember the sound of the old Routemasters revving around the backroads, the good old-fashioned buses with the open platform at the back so you could feel the crisp London breeze as you trundled along. Those were the good old days they were, when people actually talked to each other. Now, youngsters are stuck to their mobile phones and their fancy touchscreen tablets too afraid to talk to each other. What's happened to this world? A face-to-face conversation is a thing from the history books.

I don't believe in God and I don't drink; I must be the worst Irish person in the world, but I have faith in love and family and happiness and that's why now is the perfect time for me to go. With Al gone, I have nothing anymore... I don't want to be alone in the flat bored and helpless. I like watching my television, my soaps and my quiz shows. I like watching *Pointless* and listening to the questions even if I do not know the answers. I like my *Emmerdale Farm* and *Coronation Street* and *Eastenders* but I know the characters aren't real. And watching ain't the same without Al around. He wouldn't really watch, but he would half listen as he did his paperwork or fixed something on the dinner table. Now the world makes little sense to me, everything has changed and I feel empty. I don't have my grandchildren to look after or visit and help me, I have no one anymore and this journey is too much for me on my own.

I don't often think of Ireland but it seems only right to now. Might as well begin where my story starts, seeing as I know now where it's going to end. There was not much to do growing up in Donegal truth be told: churches, cows, green hills and sports fields where the boys played hurling or ran trials for county. But nothing exciting ever happened and it always seemed to rain. Every day, many times a day. My brothers and sisters appeared to enjoy their childhood, but it was different for me. I wanted to explore, I wanted to meet people, see different parts of the country, see the wider world.

I wish I could say it was a happy time, with all the freedom that living in a small town brings. My father was a doctor and part of his duties was as a medical surgeon to the American armed forces during the Second World War. He would always return with gifts: chewing gum and beer and things. Looking back, it was probably of all the free liquor that made both Ma and Pa depend on the drink. They used to throw these grand parties on Friday evenings that continued all weekend. There were always local people from the town – friends of Pa, strangers to us, staggering about and singing at the top of their lungs and doing things they shouldn't in their positions of responsibility.

My siblings weren't at all nice to me, but I got over that, I was the youngest and I was weak, an easy target I suppose. I don't like to talk about it really, hurts too much. But I remember seeing London for the first time after I ran away. All the people and hustle and bustle and even though it was new and crazy and unknown and scary, through the smog I saw freedom. Through the smog, I saw love. Al lived in the flat upstairs when I first moved to Fulham in the sixties; I had just left Ireland behind with very few possessions and nothing to my name. He caught my eye one morning as I left for work. What a brute of a man he was: rugby player, wrestler, mechanic. A simple man of great wisdom and great strength. He worked his way up from being a dishwasher in a little hotel near Marble Arch when he first arrived in the country, to doing what he really loved: working with cars, tampering under bonnets of all the different models and makes and messing about with engines.

Stuff I never did understand. He worked for British Airways for a while then moved to working for Kensington and Chelsea council. He loved working, he loved keeping busy. Worked part-time till the day he died, every Monday and Wednesday. He just couldn't let himself retire; he wouldn't know what to do stuck in the flat all day.

Unlike my family, Al wasn't scared to show me off. We used to go to Grenada every other year to see all his family, close members and distant ones. And as far as I was aware, there were no funny looks, no secret whispers behind my back, no calls for divorce, no *oh Al, you could have done better*. They treated me well as one of their own and I was accepted for who I was.

My routine with Al was uncomplicated and comfortable: wake up, cup of coffee, sneaky ciggy in the garden, morning shop, drop bags off, afternoon shop, home again, bit of tele, cook dinner, bit more tele, bed. A simple existence, the way we liked it. Without him now, I sit in his chair by the window and watch down the road leading out of the estate to see if he's on his way back from work. After all these years, I still have hope I'll see his silver Peugeot and realise suddenly that these last two years have just been one big nightmare.

It's not to say it was easy back in the day but at least we had each other. Me being Irish and Al being black it was never a walk in the park; never welcomed by the English, *no dogs, no blacks, no Irish* and the rest of it. It was hard for both of us to get a job at first, or a decent place to stay. I didn't drink then either, never have, but we were not allowed in certain pubs or bars, on our own and definitely not together. That's how it was back then, I even had to change my name to make it less Irish, Gloria was the first name I thought of and it stuck. I still felt more loved then than I do now though.

I might not be enjoying the journey today but it's always been buses for me. I don't do the underground; all the colours and lines confuse me. I remember when Mary, an old friend, the witness at my wedding, was at Ealing Hospital when she'd fallen down the stairs and shattered her pelvis. Must have been a few years ago now, but the stress of using London Underground still sticks with me. What a complete nightmare. I was planning to get a few buses across to see her at first but there was a crash in Shoreditch and all the buses had been diverted, so a man at the bus stop told me to take the tube. I wasn't sure but I walked down to Old Street, oh, it must have been over ten years ago now. I needed the black train first, but there were two different last stations and that confused me and nobody would really help. I did eventually find the train I needed but it still wasn't easy. I remember thinking that the tunnels were so small, it's a miracle we could even squeeze through. Once when we were in a tunnel, there must have been a loose connection or something because the lights in the carriage just went off. For a good five seconds too. That wasn't good for my blood pressure, I'll tell ya' that for nothing.

The 392

I managed to get on eventually, I braved it, I had already come this far, I didn't want to just go back. The driver was shouting over the tannoy *please mind the closing doors* and everyone was all squashed inside and I had my shopping trolley too because I wanted to bring Mary some bits, fruit and biscuits and things – I know more than anybody how bad hospital food can be. On the train, the driver was getting angrier and angrier *please move away from the doors!* He was shouting now, because every time he tried to drive off the train kept jolting and stopping really sharply. There was a man with tattoos all over his arms and on his fingers leaning on me. It wasn't his fault. There was nowhere else to go. Nowhere else for him to move. He had two big holes in his ears too. So every time we were about to go the train jolted hard again and some people were knocked off their feet. *How many times do I have to say it? PLEASE MOVE AWAY FROM THE DOORS!* The driver was so angry and aggressive it was scary actually. It must have happened five or six times. God knows how, but I got to Ealing Hospital and back again in the end but I haven't taken the tube since, not an experience I enjoyed at all.

I expected it of course, but I had an even bigger falling out with my family when Al and I decided to get married a few months after we met. The ceremony was a small one. Al took the morning off work, I swapped my morning shift for a late one at the hospital and we headed to the town hall in Al's old Morris Minor and we just did it. Mary was there too. It took less than an hour, no flowers, no photographers, no fuss. I signed the certificate and Al went to work in the afternoon while I cooked dinner like usual. That was that. I'm not sad about it, still the best day of my life, we had each other, we loved each other.

My trolley is blocking the aisle but no one gave up their priority seat at the front so there's nowhere for it to fit. There is a man with a bag still at the front being a nuisance. He's standing right in the way, right by the doors next to the driver; I nearly tripped over him when I got on. Why doesn't he just sit down? He's making the bus look untidy. In the seat in front of me, the man in shabby clothes is talking to himself loudly and taking pictures – but I can't see the camera. He smells really awful too. The schoolgirls are quieter now and there are passengers on their phones and everything seems strange.

It's really raining now and I didn't think to bring an umbrella, I have the hood of my raincoat though I suppose, that should be enough. I need to be able to see into the distance. As my final act, I need to make sure I can see the road ahead of me clearly. I have a rough plan, at the last stop, I'm going to get off and push my trolley to the busiest part of the nearest main road. Hopefully the journey won't be too long. I don't remember the roads around there too well, it's been years since I've been to Highbury but I'm sure I'll find a spot that'll work. I'll see the traffic speeding past, the cyclists and the motorbikes, the big buses and the lorries and the sports

The 392

cars speed on and I'll look into the distance. I'll just be able to make them out in the rain. I'll pick my target and see it coming faster my way. I'll think of Ireland and my daughter in Spain and her two little boys, my grandchildren, and I'll think of Al and I'll think about being with him again. My slippers will tiptoe to the edge of the kerb as the cars whizz on and the target approaches at speed. There is water being splashed everywhere because of the giant puddles on the road and the rain is still coming down heavy. The traffic is roaring on: engines, horns and sirens. I could jump in front of a train at the station in Highbury, it would definitely hit harder, but I prefer buses, I always have. Yes, today, no one will have to throw me under the bus I'll be able to do it myself. At last, for the first time in a long time, I'll be able to do *something* for myself. And as I move into the traffic, I'll hold the picture of Al in my hands; I always keep his picture under my blouse and close to my heart. Right here. A little one of both of us together outside the flat... but what's this hard thing here? What's *this* doing here? What a strange place to be...

It's here and it always has been. Oh Glor, what you like? There's my blasted bus pass, tucked in my bra. How silly I can be. I never used to be this forgetful but your brain starts to play tricks on you by the time you get to my age, it really does. Maybe I'm not as useless as I think. Yes, maybe there's life in this old girl yet. I know what I must have done, knowing how important it was to have it today of all days, I kept it here for safe keeping. Of course I did. I always do things like that. Put important things in safe places: precious old pictures of Al, money to pay the bills, freedom pass. It's pretty clever of me really. There must be a bit of life up there still. I made it to the bus stop, I did. I pushed my trolley and lifted it onto the bus. Did that too. And despite being scared of everything and everyone at the best of times, I spoke to the blind man and eventually found my seat. Like I used to in the old days as an NHS nurse at the worst of times, I held my own, I was brave. Maybe there is hope yet. And look, it's only just gone nine-thirty, there's still time to do some shopping, a bigger shop, one to last the week. We've past Dalston already, but I could see what the shops in Highbury have, something new for a change? Or get another bus to Angel; I used to go there all the time a few years ago. And why should it just be the basics? Why shouldn't I treat myself to a lean bit of beef, a whole bag of potatoes, a couple of carrots and ice cream with chocolate Flake for afters, oh, and why not, a bag of fudge.

I'm not as useless as I think. Even though it's raining harder now, the world outside has a different colour, like London is being washed clean, like one of those stories from the Bible I used to have to read when I was little. The shop signs shimmer, the streets glisten and everything dirty is made clean. As I look out the window and through a gap in the clouds, despite it chucking down buckets, I can see a ray of light coming through the grey skies, a glimmer of hope, Al's smile shining down? Look Glor, look how beautiful all the people look, all young and sprightly as they bob along the pavement trying to avoid getting too wet. Look at the people huddled together under the bus stop, they might look miserable now but later when the sun is shining they will smile and enjoy life again like young people should. Even the people on this bus look beautiful too, in fact, what a beauty there is sat on the other side of this bus. A young mixed-race girl. She looks strangely familiar, like someone from my past, a bit like my Maya, the same curly hair, same sparkly eyes too. There's a lovely colour to her, a healthy hue. She talks to the young boy next to her in the black and purple school uniform, there's a bit of a smile on her face like she's clearly enjoying his company. He looks younger than her, two or three years, but this is young love and it's lovely to see. They smile at each other. They hug. They hold hands. They clearly have fallen in love and my heart softens seeing them so close to me.

Maybe I'm not done with this life just yet... I know, I have an idea. I think I have my little black address book, the book with all my telephone numbers from years back, more, decades, I'm sure it's in my trolley, I'm sure it's here somewhere. You never know who you might need to call in an emergency. This is an emergency. At the bottom of this trolley I'm sure I saw it last... Here it is! I have an idea; I'm going to give Maya a call. See what she's up to, see how she's doing, check the boys are doing well too. Maybe arrange a visit? Yes, that's a good idea. Maybe

I have one last journey left in me. We could meet in France, Paris, somewhere in the middle then I won't even have to take a plane. I think there's a train you can take from Kings Cross, Val from downstairs was telling me this just the other day. I fumble with the pages, the yellowing paper melting in my fingers. I flick through the alphabet, names and numbers. Old friends, distant relatives, old doctors, and there she is. My Maya. English name, Spanish number.

I poke the man on his shoulder, it's forward of me but this is an emergency.

'Excuse me, dear, can you help me? May I use your telephone?'

I am still coming Al, but just not today.

STU

I would Diane Abbott. I would Dina Asher-Smith. I would Brenda Emmanus. I would Alison Hammond. I would Alexandra Burke. I would Clara Amfo. I would Lupita Nyong'o. I would Amma Asante. I would Serena Williams. I would Venus Williams. I would Beverley Knight. I would Nicola Adams. I would Simone Biles. I would Rihanna. I would Eniola Aluko. I would Michaela Coel. I would Ashley Banks. I would Samira Mighty. I would Dawn Butler. I would Oti Mabuse. I would Chimamanda Ngozi Adichie. I would Mica Paris. I would Michelle Obama. I would Naomi Campbell. I would FKA Twigs. I would Beyoncé Knowles. I would London Hughes. I would Kelechi Okafor. I would Grace Jones. I would Denise Lewis. I would Vivian Banks. I would Kate Osamor. I would Angelica Bell. I would Letitia Wright. I would Janelle Monáe. I would Regina King. I would Christine Ohuruohu. I would June Sarpong. I would Caster Semenya. I would the bus driver.

I'm sure this bus goes to Aqua Cunt. Or at least somewhere

near. It might be a little further up, more towards Holloway, near the stadium somewhere, past that shop that says *we-buy-any-porn.com* in big white and blue letters. It's just a nickname, Aqua Cunt, heard it said by someone once. It's Aqua something though, I'm sure. In this job, you learn lots about the local landmarks. I've never been, of course, I hear it's a seedy little place, I doubt any of the girls there would be hotter than her anyway. Why would I want a rotten disease-ridden Russian when I could have the bus driver of my dreams?

I watch on.

Moleskine out, my move will require quality planning. I have to consider the TV crew; what if they all want to interview her after she parks the bus up at the last stop? Or what if the guy at the front gets there first?

I know what I want. When we get to Highbury, I'll dally a little, pretend to be a courteous passenger slowly rising from my seat, allowing every passenger off first before bowling over and making my move. The schoolkids will have gone. The granny is shepherded off. The camera crew conduct their interviews with the MP outside in the rain. The man with the bag will have got off too, having seen she's not interested and that he's lost, and I'll be taking home the prize. It'll be just the two of us. And there she'll be, fiddling with her little card machine, or dutifully filling in one of those little cards – scribbling what time she arrived and checking what time she's due out again. I will cough to get her attention, and at first, her eyes won't leave the paper she's writing on, she will grunt an acknowledgement, so I will cough deliberately again, more purposefully, and she will look up and our eyes will meet and our hearts will ache. I won't have to say very much. She will know almost instantly what will happen next and before I even have to do anything else I'll hear the click of her cab door opening and I'll take her by the hand and lead her towards the back of the bus.

White lines off her black skin is what I want. Tonight. Back at my flat, she's lying on her back on the kitchen unit, then the sofa, then the glass dining table in the corner. Naked. Head and breast in all its beautiful black glory. Her left leg bent at the knee, right one fully outstretched, her feet arched forward to extenuate her length like a ballerina. Tights flung over the sink, shoes strewn across the floor, bra limp on the kettle. As it's a special occasion, I've got two grams of gear in. On her dark skin, I chop up the first clumps with my bank card and angle into one long line. A single route, tits via the midriff and down to her clit like a snail trail. Despite the odd playful giggle, she enjoys the challenge of trying to keep perfectly still as I roll up a twenty, tap it down on the glass tabletop to keep the paper tight and begin my descent.

She's giggling and squirming now as I kneel and begin snorting my way down. All the way, around the roundabout of her belly button and down the home straight in one. The hit is immediate. My nose twitches. Heart beats faster. Teeth numb.

Blood pressure rising. The threat of a cardiac arrest in this moment dangerously possible. I feel the hit at the back of my throat – that familiar old newspaper taste – and wash it down with the prosecco we're drinking to celebrate this coming together this evening. I sweep up the remaining residue with my middle finger and collapse onto to the settee, head light yet energised.

It's already having an effect. Within seconds I'm slouched on the sofa spouting nonsensical stories of sunsets and long walks on the beach, marriage and children. I'll have a mouth ulcer or two to deal with in the morning but for her exotic love tonight, for this magical unity, it's definitely worth it. Now it's her turn. She climbs down from the dining table and wipes the surface clean with the underside of her forearm. She cuts up a new bit, lines up the lumpy powder with the precision of a surgeon undertaking intimate surgery. She's done this before. She re-rolls my twenty, tighter, I hear the clicking of her newly-manicured sexy blue fingernails. She stands with her feet a foot apart like a footballer about to curl one into the top corner. Her angular body made up of perfectly straight lines. She smiles playfully and bends over to begin. I'm behind, observing her at work, twiddling my semi, pinching at my pre-cum, fingering the sticky liquid. My view of her now entirely obscured by her big black bum. Stretch marks like ocean waves descend her hips, a sea of sexy stories, deep dark African secrets written on scroll. She's teasing me,

I know she is, bouncing and wiggling it, every small movement exaggerated. I'm hard.

This could all be arranged so easily. I've got this great number. A Serbian-born man, he told me once when we had to delay a transaction and act normal, as we saw the blue flashing lights of a police car whizz past us while parked on Stoke Newington High Street. All you have to do is text the postcode and within seconds he gives you the OK with an e.t.a. He keeps loads of little packages of the gear in the leather bit under the gearstick. It's almost too easy, too tempting. It's good shit too, shit that makes you grind your teeth and your jaw stiff so you're gurning your face off almost straight away.

It's no secret, we all dabble, we all work hard and feel like we deserve to let our hair down every now and then. We might hit Dalston on a Friday night, go to Birthdays or Superstore and have a few drinks. Five or six of us. Tactical turns in the tiny club toilet, wiping the seat down with the bog roll, then licking the edge of a bank card and wincing at the sharpness. Furtive handshakes as the gear changes hands again. Life on the Crossrail 2 team can be hard going; everything is taking too long and nothing's officially been given the green light yet, so it's all plans, proposals and permission. We're all waiting so we can get stuck in with the fun stuff and start building the train lines and the platforms and the brand new stations.

The schoolgirls' cackle, or perhaps the enthusiastic driving down these bouncy backroads brings me back to my senses with a bump. The bus speeds up and I need to confront this mysterious man at the front. I want to turn him around, grab him by his neck and shout *Fuck off she's mine!* I want to punch him in his face, blow him up, finish him off. But I can't do a single thing, because I'm barely covering my growing erection with my notebook.

A bell rings. We've reached Newington Green and that cunt with the bag is still at the front, trying to ruin my fantasy, ruin the most perfect evening with my African queen. I feel angry and aroused at the same time. I'm going to have to say something soon; he can't get away with this brazen attempt at theft. It's wrong. I have no other option, I'm going to get up and confront him, just as soon as this boner dies down.

It's beginning to rain hard now and the windows are steaming up. A trip to Kew might have to wait after all, it's not the weather for a romantic stroll, today we'll just go back to mine and fuck till our privates are sore. The camera crew have nearly set up. The blind guy has moved seats. The crackhead is snapping away and talking to himself louder than before. I'm trying to think unsexy thoughts: Maggie Thatcher, Theresa May, The Queen, the creepy woman from the Trivago adverts. No good. It's going off down there, every thought of the driver, the sexy captain of this ship, the enslaved damsel of this fairy tale, my heart beats faster and my excitement gets harder to contain. It's ready and raging and there's only one thing I can to do about it.

The 392

This must be Canonbury now and things are getting desperate. I can't not do it now; I simply can't hold it in and let this feeling pass. I look around and over my shoulder like I'm checking my blind spot pulling out onto the motorway. A quick look is enough. It's clear. There's room for my hand to squeeze in, I stick my fingers under the elastic, I feel the rough of my pubes and bury my hand in deeper. There's definitely nobody looking. No one ever *really* looks at you in London. I feel the skin of my shaft, my protruding veins, my wet tip. I'm thinking about her black areoles – pointed with excitement – black knees, black flaps. She's shaved her legs, no in-growns. She's slipped off her loafers or Louboutins – or whatever she has chosen for the occasion – and is sliding her high-arched feet up my leg till they're rubbing up against the underside of my balls. I'm sliding off her tight, navy-blue bottom-hugging skirt with my eager hands. Her soles are peachy, fleshy, West African. She's wiggling her black toes free so I raise them to my lips and she shoves them in my mouth and I suck on them, hard. I'm licking in-between each nub, bathing each one in my saliva and watching the spit slide down the curve of her foot and around her ankle. With my drooling mouth, I add further gloss to her pink-painted toenails. I roll the tip of my tongue under each nail and suck it like the juice from fruit. I undo my shirt and she slides her feet over my chest, pinching my nipple with her big toe.

She says things as I submit to her sexiness: mean

things, nasty things: imperative, interrogative, imperative, interrogative. *Suck my toes. You like that yeah? Suck them harder. You've been a bad boy haven't you?* She reaches forward, yanks at my belt and unzips my slim-fits. She's lying across the back seats of this bus, resting her head on the window, as her size sixes make their way down my torso, wet. When my Calvins come down, she starts wanking me off with both feet, slow at first, then fast. My cock throbs. I'm pre-cuming now, more liquid added to the sloppy mix. Her earrings jangle and her face is all sweaty and focused as she slides her feet around my foreskin towards me, then towards her, up and down my shaft rhythmically, faster and faster. It's still raining outside and the windows are steaming up. The wrinkles of her sole appear and disappear as they work their magic. Up and down. Faster and faster. I'll make noises. She'll groan. I'll squirm. Veins protruding. The bus goes fast, it whizzes down Wallace Road; we're now just a few stops from the end. We're close. I'm close. I stick it in. Outside sounds aren't coming through clear, just background noise. She's biting her bottom lip: groaning, panting, screaming. We're nearly there. Visions of her eyes rolling back and her neck tilting back; she's gripping my shoulders and her nails are digging into my skin and I'm sweating, profusely. My eyes are going funny; sight is blurry. I'm trying to constrain my grimace, my breathing heavier. I still hope no one can see me like this; I'm covering the action with my coat and bag. I'm biting my bottom lip. We go over the speed bumps at speed. We overtake a 30, I think. No one knows the state I'm in; I hope they don't know the state I'm in. My thumb and index finger work in tandem, I try to stifle the shaking but it's hard, so so hard. I'm working the ridge of my helmet, the sweet spot, rubbing the ridge over and over. In my head, her legs are spread wide apart, outstretched over the back of the seats, toes gripping any handle they can find. I'm in there, thrusting away, CT Plus moquette burning my knees. It's rough, it's animalistic, it's primitive, it's beautiful. Not even a glimpse of the weirdo at the front trying to ruin everything could ruin this. Not even thoughts of his sordid intervention can stop me now. I'm so close. I feel it going all through me. Oh yes... she glances in my direction from the mirror and this is enough. Enough... I conceal my heavy breathing, my light panting and before I can say The Elizabeth Line, thick white slime gushes out the tiny slit at the end of my dick and trickles down my fingers. In my head I direct the dribble onto her expectant toes and heave back from my euphoria, panting still.

Thank you gorgeous.

We've reached Highbury already, a few stops from the end, and it's still raining heavily and there's still a mess in my trousers and there's still a man standing at the front. My fingers are sticky and I've just noticed a young girl on the bus; black(-ish), curly hair, holding her stomach, writing something on her phone and then talking with the schoolboy next to her. She's very pretty. I think I might half love her now.

DIAMOND

Ayo Jay *Your Number* is now Paigey Cakey *Boogie* on my Spotify. Paigey Cakey is so beautiful. She's mixed-race and she can rap and she's an actress; I swear, they have all the luck. She wears the nicest tracksuits and has the best kreps in her videos and her hair looks so nice too because she always gels her baby hair in such a nice way with the curly bits that are always so neat. I bet she could get any boyfriend she wants. One of her videos is filmed in Estelle's block – Estelle's so lucky, she has a photo of them together when she came to shoot her video in De Beauvoir that time, they both look so beautiful and peng like two light-skinned angels.

Me, I'm never gonna get a boyfriend, it's a fact like George shoots Lennie at the end of *Of Mice and Men* or that Henry the eighth had six wives. The boy who could have been my new boyfriend, and Kamari's new dad, has done what dads do and run off to another woman. I can see him chatting to the same girl at the front of the bus who tried to tell us to be quiet earlier. You can tell by the look on their faces that they know each other; you can see they have history, that they have a connection. I just don't understand what it is. Why don't boys like me?

Forget school today. What's the point? I'm already so late. This bus is so slow as well; it's going down all the tiny roads instead of the main roads which have the bus lanes. I have a new idea.

'Wanna go Westfields, Es?'

'What now? Diamond, we got school.'

'Oh come on, school's shit!'

She gives me a shocked confused look; she's probably never heard me swear before.

'Wow Di, look at you, you that vex?'

'I'm not vex I just don't feel like going school today.'

She jerks her head in the boy's direction. 'Don't let that wasteman piss you off, he's not even that buff.' She grabs my head with both hands. 'You're beautiful Di, no homo, don't worry you'll find a nice man soon, you just have to do what I do. Trust me.'

'I know, Es, I just don't want to go the school.'

She looks at me like she feels proper sorry for me.

'I'm worried about Mum,' I say looking down at the floor of the bus with a sad face. This is not a complete lie.

'I don't even mind you know, I'm shit at school anyway, you're the neeky one who could go uni one day.'

Even in my darkest moods, Estelle knows how to make me feel better. We have the same sense of humour basically. It feels like we're sisters sometimes, like, she often knows what I'm thinking before I say it, we even sometimes finish each other's sentences. We FaceTime each other every day for hours, talking about everything that's gone on that day. I think we'll be friends forever.

She gives a little half shrug and I know this means it's on, we'll stay on this to Highbury and take the train to Stratford and go Westfields. I don't even have much money on me but it doesn't matter, I don't really wanna go shopping today. I'm going to just hand out my phone number and Snap to boys like people hand out their CV looking for a part-time job. I'm sick of feeling so unwanted and unsexy; I want to be like Estelle, I want to be like Paigey Cakey, I just want boys to fancy me. When Mum dies, I want somebody to hold me tight and say everything is going to be OK.

I usually like school. My favourite subjects are PE and English. My English teacher is the coolest, he has this high-top like Will Smith used to have and always tries to copy the slang we use around school. He doesn't even ring home if you've been bad; he just tries to advise you to not do it again and tells us how we can all do better in life if we work hard. I think he's cool because he's young and knows what it's like for us. Mariam, who's in one of the other forms in Year 10, found his Tinder profile the other day. It's unbelievable that he doesn't have a wife already; he's pretty buff for a teacher. He's probably the only teacher I could maybe tell about Mum, I mean, if for some reason I had to.

Estelle is playing with her hair still, using her little pocket mirror to make sure her bun is well-shaped and neat. I wished my hair looked nicer than it does now. As a girl in a black family, you've got to know how to cook, clean, and look after your hair. It's the rules of the house, like no swearing, no whistling and no fizzy drinks. The other day I relaxed my hair myself but oh God it hurt so much. Mum usually does it for me but she'd been in bed all day and I didn't want to disturb her so I tried to do it myself. I had to do it then because I was meeting Estelle in Brick Lane later that day; we were gonna look at the vintage clothes and take pictures for her Instagram page. So I bought some Dark and Lovely from Pak's in Dalston and ran up straight to the bathroom when I got home while Mum was still sleeping. I poured the liquid in the small bottle with the white creamy stuff and mixed it in properly using the little wooden stick. I mixed it in till my hands were sore because that's what I was taught to do. I tried to put it in really carefully; I was concentrating so hard in the mirror, my tongue was sticking out and everything, I must have looked so silly. But after about five minutes it started to burn in places, like by the temples, and I tried to fight through the pain, but it hurt so much I had to wash it all out before the fifteen minutes it usually takes when Mum does it. When I was done, I looked in the mirror and cried. The edge of my forehead was red and sore. Half my hair was smooth like how it should be but the other half was still rough and afro-y because I didn't leave the relaxer in long enough or maybe I didn't put enough in particular areas. I didn't go to Brick Lane in the end; I looked too stupid. So I just blanked all of Estelle's messages and cooked dinner for Mum and Kamari instead, the saltfish was probably saltier than it should have been.

I'm sort of clever and I have good predicted grades, but Estelle knows how to work a room. I think this means when all eyes are on you when you enter a class like in History or Science. There's something about her personality which attracts people like magnets. My breasts are biggish but her breasts are bigger, my bum *is* big but her bum is bigger. To be honest, I just want to look like the girls on the Instagram explore page; I want to have toned abs and nice clothes and hair that's always on point. I want more followers too so everything I post online will get many likes.

I want to look like Amelia Monet and be the baddest, the baddest. I just want nice nails, and a nose-piercing and a boyfriend to take me to Vue in Angel and buy popcorn, pick-'n'-mix and nachos and then treat me to Five Guys or Wagamamas. And because I don't know how to use chopsticks, he'll ask the waitress for a fork from the kitchen at the back because he's nice like that. When we're done, we walk down

Upper Street but stop to look through the window of Foxtons at all the posh houses that cost millions. With our bellies full and our hearts pumping we get the 394 back to Hoxton and he'll kiss me on the lips. I don't have to give him a blowjob yet because he doesn't want to rush things. I sit on my bed that night, zooming in on his Snapchat photo and kissing the picture of his face goodnight, dreaming about me and him getting married and having beautiful babies before screen goes black.

The strange man is still at the front with the bag on his back and no one is doing anything about it. No one has called the police and the driver isn't saying anything either. The Grove boy that I thought might have been into me, is still talking to the girl at the front who's light skinned, of course. What am I doing wrong? I licked my lips the way Estelle does, I was kinda rude to him, the way Estelle is to boys, I've got my contact lenses in, I even had a glass of water yesterday because I wanna be more healthy, and clear some of my spots.

I swear these days I can't even watch TV without thinking about boys. Estelle slept over my house the other day and we watched this programme called *Naked Attraction* on Channel 4. We stayed up so late just to watch it because people in school were saying it was proper disgusting. So Estelle and I bought Doritos and M&Ms from the Co-Op and waited up to see what all the hype was about. Mum was sleeping upstairs so she didn't know we were watching it. It was the weirdest programme I had ever seen. Basically, it's a dating show where you decide who you most want to have sex with by looking at their willies and fannies. Me and Estelle were just creasing with laughter every time they showed a close-up of their private parts, some of them looked so odd I swear, like I didn't even know that they look like that, they were all so different as well. We Snapchatted everything of course, it was such a funny night. I still couldn't believe my eyes. I never knew penises could look so strange, Estelle says Ty has a normal one, but none of them I saw on the programme looked normal to me. Watching it made me think that I just want a boyfriend with a nice normal dick. We stopped watching when the bisexual guy came on because being bisexual is greedy and that's a sin, so we watched *The Pursuit of Happyness* instead to remind us of Mr. Harris our English teacher and because Jaden Smith is so cute in it.

Now I look at her properly, I swear I kinda recognise the girl that boy's chatting too. The girl who told us to be quiet before. I'm sure I've seen her before, someone's Snap maybe. Estelle will know.

'Estelle, I swear I recognise the girl that boy's talking to.'

Estelle stops patting the front of her hair for a second to have a little look.

'Who, the girl at the front? Yeah, that's that Natalie chick innit.' She's so casual as she speaks, like she knew that the whole time, she just has a little peek and carries on playing with hair in her little pink pocket mirror. 'She looks alright though still for a pregnant girl,' she adds.

'She's pregnant? How do you know everything?'

'Yeah, that boy, or should I call him *your man's* older brother is the dad.'

So that's how they know each other; that's why they're so close, it all makes sense now suddenly. It's mad that this Grove boy who chatted to me is the younger brother of this Natalie girl's unborn baby. Sometimes drama in the ends is like an episode of *Hollyoaks*.

'So you knew the boy as well? Why didn't you say anything?' I say annoyed.

'Alright Di, it's not that deep.'

'Do you know the whole of Hoxton or something?'

'I know people innit. I know he'll be vex he's speaking to her.'

'Who?' I ask.

'The older brother obviously,' she says.

'So, go on, what else do you know?'

'Chill Di, shh your mouth, you're making it so bait.'

'What's the brother's name? Have you got his number?'

'Yeah, Roman something, probably on WhatsApp, I think.'

The man is still at the front with his darkish-green bag on his back. I think it says No Fear, some dead brand that you can buy in Sports Direct. He looks all strange in his dead clothes and with something I can't quite see but is being fiddled with in his hands. His beard is all long and fluffy too like those suspects that you see on the news. If it was trimmed a bit around the edges like DJ Khaled or Rick Ross or something maybe it wouldn't be so weird but his is all wild like animal fur. Maybe Estelle is right and he is a terrorist and we should all be worried. My form tutor did say that we have to be extra vigilant because of all the things that's been going on recently, but how do you really know what people are terrorists? You can tell everyone is sort of watching him, they don't know either.

'So you have his number on WhatsApp, yeah?' I ask.

'Who, Roman?'

'Yeah. Tell him... tell him his own younger brother is trying to chirpse his girl.'

'Diamond, that's kinda badmind.'

'Tell him!'

'Boy, say nothing, it's only 'cos you're my girl innit.'

She gets her phone out and writes the message quickly, and after a few seconds I see the ticks which meant it's definitely been sent. At that moment, I feel like an oxymoron, happy and sad at the same time, I learned that word in English, Mr. Harris told me it.

BOXER

'Boxer,' she says. It's Natalie. And I swear for a moment, as I look into her big brown eyes and see her long eyelashes fluttering up and down like the butterflies in my stomach, the world seems to slow down and this weird feeling comes over me like I'm about to sneeze.

'Thought it was you,' she says. 'What's good?' Up close, she looks amazing, so buff and kind and sweet.

She's been to the flat before, like when she comes round late at night to secretly see my brother and she always looks decent. But usually it's dark and she's wearing my brother's extra-large Ellesse hoodie so you can't really see how banging her body is. Today she looks so beautiful. It's strange that she's my brother's babymother; he should feel so lucky to have a good-looking girl like her. Obviously, I don't know the full story but even if something bad did happen, I still wouldn't treat her like he does. That's too deep.

Her hair is long and curly, her skin is soft-looking and

brown like the inside of a Snickers, her body looks curvy in the right places even though there's a baby in her belly – you can tell she used to work out, play sport and go to the gym and that. She looks good, like a girl you would proudly take to KFC or a house party in the ends or shopping in Stratford. She's wearing a little leather jacket and a Supreme t-shirt. She should probably be wrapped up warmer in her condition, but I'm sure she knows what she's doing. *What's good?* She said. I wish I could reply with something smart or something cool but I can't get the nice words out because I'm all shy and nervous. 'Good, well, not bad. You?' I don't really know what to say, I know people are watching.

'Yeah same, just a bit...' She looks down at her stomach. 'Pregnant.'

I smile a shy smile and lick my lips nervously. She's absolutely beautiful, I can't stop thinking that. The most perfect girl I have ever seen and I'm just staring at her thinking what an idiot my brother is for treating her like this. My heart is all weird as I stand here in the middle of the aisle, I feel a bit awkward. My face feels all hot too like I've just had a fresh trim with a shape-up from Scrapey and it still stings around the edges a bit. Or even worse, when the barber sprays that strong hairspray stuff in your face after he's finished cutting it and you can't even open your eyes. In the seat in front, there's a guy with his hands down his trousers, it looks like he's playing with himself but I can't really tell if he's actually rubbing one out. That's proper grim if he is. There's the guy at the front still, with his dead bag and his dead baggy jeans and the dead kreps. There's a blind man sat next to a black man with a nice suit on in the seats behind Natalie. There's an old lady with her shopping trolley sat behind me. Then there's me, standing awkwardly in the middle, not knowing my next move.

'I feel bad about all this. My brother is acting kinda deep.' My words are slow and serious, so she knows I actually mean it, as if to let her know I wouldn't have treated her this way if the tables were turned around. The bus goes so fast now like this thing I saw on ITV the other week, it was about this bus that had a bomb on it and if the bus went below a certain speed the bus would blow up.

There is a long pause between us. Like the conversation is loading or like when you're watching *Stranger Things* on Netflix and the internet is crap and the people are all blurry and you can't make out what's really going on for the first two minutes. Then, as I'm about sit down next to her, my phone vibrates in my pocket. Even though my screen is all cracked I can still see who it is, my big brother. My heart feels a different kind of funny now, I know when he rings it's never a good thing. I can't just air him though, that would make him more angry, so I'm forced to answer. The spit I swallow feels like a rock going down my throat.

'*Hey... 'sup?*' I choose my words so carefully, like my tongue is a shank and I've got to be careful how I use it before I cut all the insides of my mouth up.

'I hear you're on that bus with that sket,' he says, his voice is angry and aggressive; he's on one I can tell, he's not fucking about. It's mad how fast news travels in the ends. I have to think fast myself now; Natalie's trying to not look like she's just waiting for the conversation to come to an end. She's writing something on her phone, I can't tell whether it's a text or a note or something. Whatever it is, it looks long, like a story.

'It's not a good time to talk. I'm on the bus innit.' I'm trying to keep the situation calm but my heart is beating bare fast and my legs feel heavy like I've just run the hundred metres and I could faint. I know this is bad and he's gonna do something.

'Listen to me.' He's getting really mad now, it sounds like he's speaking through gritted teeth. *'Me and the boys are coming Highbury now, keep her on the bus till you get to the last stop, you hear me?'*

'What, now?'

'I can't let that sket have that baby. Don't fuck this up.'

'What you gonna do?'

'I can't let that sket have that baby,' he says again and hangs up. Shit! This is bad. What am I gonna do? I look at her; she can probably see the worry in my face. I picture my brother and his boys ganging up on her and threatening her, wearing ballys, swearing and spitting at her. They'll tell her to get rid

of the baby or they'll do it for her. They'll push her to the floor and put a knife to her neck or a hammer to her belly and they'll tell her to get an abortion or they'll kill her and then ride off on peds. Stolen ones on fake plates.

My brother has gotten into some bad shit recently. Drugs. Robberies. All organised gang stuff. He was telling me all this just the other day. He goes out with his boys on Cally Road and Holloway and starts looking for peds to steal, sometimes they have to go as far up as Archway and Highgate or Crouch End. They find a target, usually a Deliveroo driver, and rob them at knifepoint. They seem to always get away with it too. Their new thing is MacBooks. He told me he gets five bills for each Mac on the street and they're so easy to get in Islington, everyone's got one. Go into any coffee shop or café and you'll find ten, twenty people typing away on their Airs and Pros. I asked him why he does it to those people, and he told me 'cos they can obviously afford to buy another, we can't. He does it on the daily. He's on the rob for laptops at about lunchtime and iPhones and expensive headphones like Beats, Sony, Bose or even Marshall from about nine. Not Kindles though, they're dead. Niggers don't read. Sometimes they target a person on their way home from work or the gym or whatever and just wait till they take their phone out and BAM! That's when they attack, do a U-ee in the middle of the road and ride on the pavement. The person at the back grabs it quick and puts it in the side-bag and they speed off weaving in-between the cars and riding through the estate with another new iPhone to add to their collection. Easy. Not even Operation Venice got them shook. It's all carefully planned; it's like they're predators from one of the shows that that guy David Attenborough presents. He has even told me that they've carried acid before too, in Lucozade bottles, but said he has never actually used it on anybody. But every time I see a news report of another acid attack in London, I get this bad feeling in my stomach and I just hope he hasn't been lying to me.

He's only a couple of years older than me but everyone says we're basically like twins 'cos we look so similar, but he's more ghetts than I am. And I know he does some bad things, but he's still my brother, so I have to support him even when he makes stupid mistakes. But I know this time he's gonna do something really bad to Natalie and inside a big part of me feels like I can't just sit back and let him.

'Everything good?' she asks, her eyes all big and shiny. My head feels light and empty and my lips feel dry. I swerve the question like when I'm walking and quickly try to avoid walking through 'batty man's legs', which is basically one of them big road signs with two poles holding it up. Walking through one means you like sucking man's dick.

'Let me sit here for a bit... before I fall.'

I sit down and even though it's raining outside and there is a strange man at the front everyone seems to be focused on, my heart feels warm sitting next to her and then I get thinking. She's got everything going for her looks-wise. She's like one of them girls from Fredo's *Ay Caramba* video, the one where they're all in their bikinis bouncing their bums up and down and looking all peng. She's nineteen now I think, there's just three years difference between us. It could work, we could have a future, you know, nice walks in the park, maybe even a baby of our own together. It'll be a bit strange in the beginning, but it won't matter, we'll get used to it. This could be the beginning of something exciting, better than passing my GCSEs or pinging a free-kick into top bins for the school team, I think this is what love feels like.

I want to get away from gangs and my brother and moped muggings and walking stupidly in the dark like Conor McGregor with my arms swinging to look hard. The other day, must have been last Thursday or Friday, I thought I heard someone get shot in the ends again so I ran but I think it was just a firework. My heart was beating so fast, I thought I was gonna have a heart attack. I swear, every time I hear fireworks in the ends around this time of the year I'm so shook in case it's someone with a gun. I don't want to live like this anymore, too stressful. I look at Natalie and then put my hand on her thigh because it feels right to; I want her to know that everything is going to be alright.

'Family matters,' I say, grabbing her hand.

And as I look around at the people on the bus like the crackhead taking another fake picture, the useless-looking camera crew, the blind guy with the stick and the football top talking to the black guy in the smart suit and shiny loafers with the tassels that I clocked earlier, and the old lady with her shopping trolley, I know I can't live like this, with all this stress anymore. In this city, on these roads it's hard to make inroads. I think about how life could be, Natalie and me and the baby away from all of this drama and crime and grime and trapping. I want to get away from Hackney and Islington and London, rent a little place outside of the city like Borehamwood or Watford, where my boy Joseph lives maybe, one of them cottages with a nice garden. Get a dog. I could get a little job, something small like Subway to start or use my bike and work for Uber Eats or Deliveroo in the evening. I bet there's no moped crime in somewhere like Norwich. Or leave England altogether, go Paris or Dubai or Abu Dhabi and live tax free with a nice car and a nice house with a swimming pool. I'm seventeen next May. We could get away from my brother and the man at the front today because what if he is a terrorist, what if there is a bomb in his bag? What then?

I feel Natalie looking at me. I've always kinda sensed there's been a connection between us. She's holding my hand, which is kinda shaking, and puts her fingers in-between mine. Her fingers are smooth. I look at her, and we sort of have this moment. It's hard to explain. We both know it's wrong and we shouldn't feel this way about each other, but right now, I don't care about nothing else. I should tell her what's going down, you know, what my brother is planning to do, but I can't do that either. I can feel the softness of her skin and my heart is racing and whatever happens I'm not gonna let either of them get hurt. Her or the baby. I can't.

BARNEY

I sit down again. The old lady's shopping trolley was in the way, right in the middle of the aisle, and not being graced with the slenderest of frames these days, I aborted mission, I false-started, did a sheepish U-turn to my seat at the back.

The strange fellow at the front fumbles about suspiciously so I think dirty thoughts to keep me calm; some dirty grime and music how it should be. I think of AJ Tracey. Bonkaz. Cadet (R.I.P). DigDat. EO. Fredo. Giggs. Headie One. Izzie Gibbs. J Hus (free my G). Krept and Konan. Little Simz. M I S to the fucking T. Novelist. Oscar #Worldpeace. President T. Russ. Stormzy. The Streets on tour with Tonga. Unknown T. Vic Santoro. Wiley. Xavier Unknown. Youngs Teflon. Zags.

All of them.

I look out the window. I look out beyond De Beauvoir. The rain falling heavier now.

I see the City workers in trench coats clutching Bodum travel mugs full of Tassimo-made coffee, pounding it down the road to get to the office by ten having dropped little Oscar off at the childminders. The bookworms clutching *The Lonely Londoners* and *Lincoln in the Bardo* who'll get on a packed bus to Old Street and jump on the tube to their offices, a small literary agency in central somewhere, followed by the British builders with bloated bellies and this morning's *Metro* folded under their arm, man-handling their paint-stained toolboxes. The dwindling Eastern Europeans have trekked across the city already and have been on site since sunrise; they neck cans of Relentless like they're drinking Zubr. London is open. #LondonIsOpen. A London growing year on year: an army of grafters grinding to keep the city moving. Haggerston swimming baths is still closed and black people still can't swim. Haggerston swimming baths will become shops, community spaces and offices and black kids still won't learn to swim. Black kids can't go surfing down in Newquay on GCSE results day with Tom, Aron and Jeremy because black kids still can't swim, but they can now shop in Haggerston and use the community spaces.

Space is at a premium. On every corner a new-build is being built: one bedroom, small outside space, good transport links, thirty per cent deposit, fixed mortgage for the first three years, six months of stamped bank statements, credit checks, get this signed by the solicitor at the end of the Victoria Line, valued at half-a-million, low interest rate, housing associations and key worker discounts. Bills not included.

I could have, I *should* have done something about this.

Over there, builders' merchants and removal businesses have been priced out and replaced by cafés and fancy flower gardens. The leisure centre is in danger; Crossrail 2 is coming. The primary school has changed its name to reflect the change and attract parents from the wider realms of the catchment area. Yummy's Café and Barry's Locks look scared. A cluster of Santander bikes sit ready to be taken for a ride along the network of new Cycle Super Highways. The Hunter S with porn pictures in the men's toilet and Hackney pale ales on tap and a barwoman with cropped hair who's come down from York to chase her dreams of going to art school during the day, Central Saint Martins. She wears a vintage Adidas t-shirt bought from Beyond Retro in Stoke Newington, gets a small tattoo of a ballerina on the underside of her arm, a homage to the dance lessons she took between the ages of six and eight. Moves from Stockwell to Cricklewood to Southall to Leyton. Dabbles in a lesbian relationship but will maybe meet a decent (enough) man one day and have a normal (enough) nuclear family to keep her parents happy. Doubt that though. Drinks pints of Kapow!, has a Twitter profile of the Neutral Milk Hotel's *In the Aeroplane over the Sea* album cover. Listens to Gus Dapperton and asks punters whether they've heard Ghostpoet's new record? She has a few piercings, one nose, three in the ears, two on the right, one on the left and a tragus that's infected and struggling to heal.

The 392

New London. New high-rise tower blocks yards from million-pound-plus houses; the sky is dark and the rainclouds don't look like budging. The man at the front with the bag and the beard does not look like budging. He's there still, perched at the front of the bus like a martyr. See it. Say it. Sorted. Outside, under the surface of aesthetic comfort – decent attire and decent hair – are uncomfortable overdraft balances, temptingly attractive payday loan adverts and difficult discussions with line managers. I still don't understand why checking your credit score could affect your credit rating. *Thanks Mum for the petrol money, but I've had to sell the Civic, no point having a car in London. Got a quick sale, I think I'll get a bicycle instead. And a good lock, I'm gonna need a good lock around here.*

Not much passenger turnover between Hoxton and Dalston and Dalston and Highbury, the passengers on now are here for the long run. There used to be a Mildway Park Station just here. Might be a good idea to rebuild it, call it Newington Green, (might be worth fixing the Overground too. Why does it go so slow?) and accommodate the new wave of trendy hipsters with their bellies full from avocado on toast breakfasts and baked eggs with avocado for lunch. *Do you have avocado ice cream? Is this suitable for vegetarians? Is this suitable for vegans? I'm a vegan too now you know. Yeah, I get my protein from nuts. Get my protein from seeds. I haven't eaten meat in three weeks now. Could you put your Mac away please sir, we don't want computers used here on the weekend, it's not the vibe we're going for.* New Balances, cropped trousers and it's getting colder and the 73 doesn't go to Victoria anymore. And I know I'm rambling but times are getting desperate and the man is still at the front I don't want to die today; I need some Krept and Konan and a little bit of Chip to make all this slightly better.

The wait goes on, still not set up, still no interview. The bus turns left then right, following the curve of a sodden jogger running alongside on the pavement. Everyone has taken up running, £40-plus to enter this race, slight discount if affiliated to a club. People put it on their Monzo. A little jog on a Sunday around the Marshes or Clissold Park to run off the hangover. Late night last night in Oslo or the Motown night at Moth Club. Run down the canal to Victoria Park, do a lap and come back. Highbury Fields 5k Parkruns and don't forget your barcode. *Well done on a new PB* automated text. *I've signed up for the Hackney Half and the Adidas Shoreditch 10k; let's grab brunch afterwards. Blimey, it was so hot wasn't it? I could barely keep up with the pacer. At least it was mostly flat, just some slight inclines by the Olympic Park. Clapton are playing Sporting Bengal at the Old Spotted Dog in the Essex Senior this week if you fancy it.*

Football kits stuffed in rucksacks, happy to play 5-a-side after work midweek, not so keen on 11-a-side anymore. Playing that team from Tottenham with all the young black boys smoking weed on the touchline was no longer fun. And over there is Acoustic café. I still have my poppy on, and people are wearing white 'Peace' poppies this year. And, I had a ticket to see Bugzy Malone last week at The Forum. And she's had her phone stolen outside The Alma and he's had his phone stolen outside The Stag. One person in the cubicle at once, we have a strict 'No drug' policy and thieves are known to operate in the area so please look after your belongings. They'll probably give Lovebox a miss this year, but Field Day and Citadel look fun. *Have you see the line-up for All Points East yet*? Or maybe Primavera, a cheeky trip to Barcelona. Tote bags of different colours and Amy's got a blue Fjallravan Kankan rucksack and Rachel has a yellow Fjallravan Kankan rucksack. And they've got a cat at home they've called Hemingway and the cat litter needs changing again, the flat is starting to stink. And they've seen an advert to do a short course at City University and maybe there's more to life for them than being an over-worked teacher and marking P.E.E paragraphs. What about that book they've always thought about writing? Turn that idea into a novella. That novella into a novel.

Winter is here. Winter Wonderland is coming. 'Wenger Out' then, but Wenger's long gone now. Sauntering smokers of flavoured vapes: strawberry and mint. She's the model from the Made adverts on the tube I think. Who would have guessed that 21 Savage was born in East? *Top of the Pops* is now *Sounds Like Friday Night* and the BBC studios aren't in White City anymore. Are they? The green hearts of Grenfell broken.

I could have, I *should* have done something about it.

Canonbury.

Every other person is wearing Patagonia and have borrowed their friend of a friend's Netflix account details to binge watch the next best thing and tweet about it. They all have witty, sarcastic Twitter bios. *Did you read that Guardian article, the one about mental health?* Round here looks like a scene from McFadden's Cold War; everyone is sick of single-use plastics. His Yé is different to her Yé but he slid into her DMs anyway and so for him, life is getting quite exciting. A neck tattoo doesn't necessarily make him a criminal. We've got section 60, stop and search in full force now.

It's a case of signed packages to work because there's no one to sign for them at home and a Saturday trip to the sorting office on Cally Road isn't ideal. A Saturday trip to the sorting office on Cally Road isn't safe because of the moped-enabled crime. Weekends are for runs, walks and birthday brunches at the Fig & Olive with bottomless prosecco. He's having his thirtieth at the Busey Building and she's booked a room downstairs at Victory Mansions. We could pass by one and dance to Toploader *Dancing in the Moonlight* then drop by the other and share a ViaVan home from Peckham and have drunk anal sex. And after, wash our sticky hands with Waitrose ginger and clementine hand wash. She looks sexy in the Boomerang video on Insta, posted this morning from last night, she's shaking her bum: she's shaking her bum, she's shaking her bum, she's shaking her bum. The two-second video plays over and over. She's shaking her bum. She's shaking her bum. She's shaking her bum. She is shaking her bum. Double-tap love heart like. There's an emoji now for every occasion. She does yoga. Competent with all of the poses: downward-facing dog and lotus onto a child pose and does a bit of Bikram too. Then a brisk walk home via Little Waitrose to get a dinner for two and Savse super green smoothies, wearing wireless headphones and listening to a playlist made up of Zara Larsson, Taylor Swift and Sigrid. Even though it's Christmas soon, she's braved a pair of open-toed heels. The ones with the gap at the back, exposing the fleshy bit of her sole. Moved down to the city a few years ago, managed to get a decent price for a flat in Homerton, ex-council. Did it up brick by brick. Developers chomping at the bit to get a bit of her Homerton land. The Overground station. The new-builds. The brand new academy. The hospital. Chats Palace. Sunday markets. Artisan bakeries. New Nike store on Morning Lane. And this is London. Fads, fashions and expense.

The bus waits to pull out.

With each turn comes great change. A London on its own journey. Working women who went to Oxford but are too ashamed to say they went to Oxford, the twenty-somethings, the start-ups, the City workers, the million-pound house owners, the renters, the council-flat livers, the dossers, the squatters, the content but not quite happy, the happy but not quite safe, the people left behind. Beautiful women with hot legs, fucked-up bottom teeth and red wine lips. It's all Brexit and Donald Trump has retweeted this and '*Oh Jeremy Corbyn!*' and Momentum and anti-austerity marches. Let's meet in the pub first, protesting makes me thirsty: two gin and tonics, three pints and a few packets of crisps. And the man is still at the front and the mood is too tense for an Instagram story, or a Facebook live video, or a WhatsApp what's-it.

I think finally the camera crew are ready, the wires have been untangled and the microphone has been set up. What is the point anymore? Is there enough time? We're all about to die, in a matter of minutes.

'Excuse me dear, can you help me? May I use your telephone?'

DEAN

Is it safe? Is it ever safe? You can never be sure; sometimes it's hard to tell. Sometimes it's worse than you think it's going to be and the clean-up... operation, shall we say, is a big one. Other times it's OK, it just passes and everything turns out fine and you think *what was all that stress about?* But it's a tough one to call today. I feel it inside me, rumbling away, it's such a heavy weight, Louis. Should I risk it? I mean, I've shat myself before, you get used to it. When you eat the shit I eat on the street, it's bound to get messy sometimes. I'll hold it in for now if I can, hopefully I can reach Highbury safely.

S*nap, snap, snap.* Let me tell you now, these shots are going to look so good. It's gonna be a book that's gonna win me awards, Louis, international recognition, prizes and prize money. The Nobel Prize of Photography or the Booker Prize for Photography, that sort of thing. I can picture it already. As the years have gone by, you can't deny I've got better and better at my craft, if I do say so myself. I'm better with angles and lighting, capturing the best in people, of all colours too: black, white, yellow, I'm managing to get it right now, play to people's strengths. If only I could show you these pictures, Louis. If only I had an actual camera like these BBC lads. That is some nice bit of kit I must say. Next week, God willing, I will get the camera I was telling you about from Cash Converters and everything will be OK.

This bus is the perfect backdrop. It's so full of character – and characters – today. The camera crew, the young girl in the flashy leather jacket, the schoolkids, the man with the bomb in his bag. There's so many different stories to tell and that's why I love photography. You're a man of culture, Louis, you understand. I've got a real talent. I'm not stupid or naïve, I read the papers: *Metro*, *Evening Standard* and *Time Out*.

Let me tell you one thing I've learned, all these Romanians coming into the country, they're not here to find proper work. Trust me, Louis, I know. I was speaking to this one fella the other day, name was Danny Petrescu or something, and he tells me that they're here to pay off their debts. They have debts they have to pay to big gangsters back home for getting them into the country in the first place. He told me himself that he owes £12,000. Twelve grand! That's a hell a lot of money, Louis. Even for guys working in the City, that's a lot of money. You'd have to beg till you're eighty years old to get anywhere near that on the street. But these Romanians make it harder for us hard-working English, Louis. When the Irish are fighting the Romanians and the Romanians are fighting the Polish. It makes us English rough-sleepers look bad. I'm not a scrounger, Louis. I'm not a second-class citizen, I've just had a bit of bad luck in life, you understand? I might not pay 5p for a plastic bag when I go into Tesco, but I'm a good person, Louis. And I'm trying to sort my life out now, get myself a proper career so I can afford to buy nice things and get out of this mess.

Where does my journey start? Well, where should I begin, Louis? There isn't really a good place to start a sad story is there? I tried to use the systems, Louis, I really did. I can read, I can write. I filled in all the forms, sat in the waiting rooms, spoke to person after person, I did every bloody assessment under the sun, Louis, honest I did. It was always the same: *just be patient Mr. Russell, it should be sorted in the next few days*. It never really was. Details were taken but nothing ever really happened, just a load of empty promises and as the days went by, and the weather got colder, I soon realised, Louis, the only person looking out for me was me. In their eyes, I was just a single bum with no kids and no qualifications; I was at the bottom of every list. No chance in hell of getting a flat, or the benefits I needed. I don't blame the workers behind the counter, Louis, you understand. It's the systems. Tanisha with the plaited purple hair, clicking away on the computer with her long purple nails is the little person in all this. It's the government that don't care. It's the government that don't do enough for people like me that have fallen on hard times. I understand that. I know now, it's a dog-eat-dog world out there, and you got to look after number one.

All I needed was a chance, Louis. Especially after the accident. I needed help. I was in a dark place for a long time after that day. You wanna know what happened? I'll tell ya'. I was hit by a bus actually: May 4th 2007. A bus much bigger than this too. A double-decker on its way to Archway. I remember the day so clearly, Louis. I was meeting my mate for a pint at the The Bank of Friendship on Blackstock Road. He's a Gooner and it's an Arsenal pub so we always used to meet there. I was walking up through Highbury Fields, even when I could afford to travel I always walked everywhere back then, I was healthier because of it too. I went up Highbury Barn, super posh, and carried on up towards Blackstock Road. I was running a bit late and I didn't want to keep my friend waiting too long, so quickened my step a bit, I was basically jogging, Louis. I was in such a good mood too, I remember I was whistling a tune that's how happy I was, when all of a sudden, I'm literally yards from the pub at this point, I see this bus, a big double-decker, coming towards me so fast. I've seen drivers speed down the hill here before, the one by the old Arsenal stadium, but I could tell this weren't right; it was swerving all over the place, Louis, like a wild animal totally out of control. It hit a kerb first, careered across to the other side of the road, and I tried to get out of way, I really did, Louis, but

I couldn't adjust my feet quickly enough; it skidded towards my direction and I knew I was in trouble. I don't remember the impact to be honest, but I woke up a few days later in Whittington Hospital, numb.

My addiction started from that day to be honest. The pain just wouldn't go away. I'd broken my shoulder, my legs, and suffered significant trauma to the head the doc said. What did I do next? It's a typical sad story ain't it? You can see for yourself, I'm not gonna lie to you. It's been a long road back and there's still a long way to go. No, I'm not clean yet. But let's just say I'm not as filthy as before, I'm a stronger person now. When you've been through what I've been through, you just have to find a way to carry on because you know it can't really get much worse.

Like many men who sleep rough on these streets, I had a dog once. Loyal little thing he was, good old Max, my red nose pit. Yeah yeah, I know what you're probably thinking, status dog, but I had him ever since he was a pup and he was as good as gold. It wouldn't have been my first choice of breed, I know they don't have the best reputations, but as soon as I saw him, I knew he was the one for me. Got him from this crazy crackhead on Murray Grove, desperate for half a gram, so we did a swap, she got the gear, I got Max and we were both happy for a while.

These streets are lonely, Louis, and having Max's company saved my life when I was at my worst. We used to get stopped by the police at least twice a day 'cos he was a pit and I was a just a tramp in their eyes; they'd threaten to take him away from me but I wouldn't let 'em. Wouldn't leave my side, we were partners in crime, literally sometimes. But this one guy had a problem with us clearly. He's known in Hoxton, he has quite a distinctive style shall we say, always wearing sunglasses whatever the weather, big beard, greying at the edges, black waistcoat, black cowboy boots. Proper weirdo. He's always inside Hoxton Gardens necking cans of the extra-strength stuff with his giant German Shepherd. There's a bit of colour to him, half-Indian maybe. You know what he did, Louis? You sure you wanna hear it?

So this guy with the sunglasses, waistcoat and cowboy boots, comes up to my bench one day where I was sitting in the Gardens having a little drink and tells me that Max should have a muzzle on. I look at him all confused. He's doing no one no harm I tell him. I'm telling you, Louis, all he was doing was sitting there, watching people go up and down the market. It was a Saturday, I remember, and the market was busy, like it used to be all the time back then. He liked doing that, he was always such an alert little thing, but he wouldn't hurt a fly, Louis, my Max, but this fella wouldn't let it go. Go somewhere else, you're not welcome, he was saying now. You don't own Hoxton Gardens I tell him and all of a sudden he gets all up in my face and gobs one right in my mouth. Phlegm and everything. I could feel his thick saliva slide down my face,

Louis. Do you know how disgusting that is? So my instant reaction was to nut him; to my surprise I caught him clean, I did. I've never head-butted anyone before, but I nutted this guy good. And you know what? It felt great. There was blood everywhere in seconds. He stumbled away all groggy, probably all shocked, calling me *fucking this* and *cunt* that.

So anyway, a couple of days later, I'm sitting in Shoreditch Park having a little drink and watching the buses go along the New North Road with Max, it's just a thing we did. The 76 to Waterloo. The 21 to Lewisham. The 141 to Palmers Green. All going to different places all over this giant city. It must have been about nine, maybe a bit later – it was dark, and I should have really started making my way back to my squat just off the Whiston Road at the time. But I was enjoying watching the buses go by this evening, wondering where all the people were going and making up stories in my head about their lives. All of a sudden, out of the shadows, these two men walk over and ask me for a light. No one asks me for a light, Louis. Never. You know, it's usually the other way round ain't it? So I had my back up straight away, I held on to Max's lead so tight, I knew something weren't right, had this feeling. Before I could try and say something and act smart, one of the guys punched me in the stomach and the pain was so bad, Louis, it travelled up and all over. I was winded straight away, gasping for breath and everything. I was doubled over and the one guy just kept pounding me, he was proper slugging at me hard. He had blue bootcut jeans on and a pair of Lonsdale trainers, the ones with the Velcro. Even though it was really dark I remember seeing them clearly because his trainers were white and my head was so close to his feet 'cos he had punched me to the ground. From the floor, I could hear Max was barking and barking because he was distressed and he was such a kind dog, Louis, he wouldn't have known what to do. Then all of a sudden, Max let out this whimper like he did when he was a li'l pup and I knew straight away they'd hurt him bad. And even though I was in so much pain and it was pretty dark, I could just about see that he was being kicked over and over by the other guy. Next thing I know, I see the guy who's been messing with Max, pull back his leg – with Max still whimpering in pain at this point as well – let fly with a huge punt with his black cowboy boot with the metal studs. And like one of those cheap footballs you get in those little corner shops, off Max flew into the distance. I couldn't believe it. Then as cool as you like they just walked off, laughing and swearing, swigging on their K ciders like proper callous cunts.

Once I came to my senses, I stumbled over to where I could hear Max panting but I could see that the poor thing was in so much pain, he was just there lying on his side and wheezing with his eyes only half open. His neck all twisted and bent out of shape. Even though I was in so much pain myself, I knelt down, right by his mouth and gave him a little kiss. His breath was so warm in the cold air, I had to put the poor thing out of his misery, so I looked around for the nearest big rock I could find.

So there we have it; that was that. Grim ain't it? It's definitely not been easy.

Snap, snap, snap.

Nearly there now, Louis, I've been there before. I'm sure she'll be fine today; she says her solicitor seems nice. Lewis was it? Or Levi maybe? Or Louis? No... that's you! I won't go inside the court itself. I'll wait outside, but I just want her to know that I'm there for her. I've been to court a few times, it's usually not as bad as you think but it's still not a nice feeling. The magistrates look at you like you're the scum of the earth sometimes but there's nothing you can do about that, it's the way of the world for people like us, Louis. That's a fact now ain't it? You can't deny that.

Nearly there now. The man is still there, isn't he? He's not moving even though he's in the way at the front there. He's not budging a bit. He still has his rucksack on, it's all pointy and bulging out like it's been packed badly and is about to explode. There's definitely something in there. Something heavy, something hard, a weight he's struggling to carry. I take more pictures... *snap, snap, snap*. I can see the big bulge, can you Louis? I wonder what it is. I need to keep taking pictures, even if we don't survive, I bet my camera will. You hear stories of black boxes surviving plane crashes don't you? Technology always lives on, Louis, even after we've gone technology continues.

Snap, snap, snap.

My stomach feels funny, rumbly and odd. Something's wrong. Did you hear that? Oh my, Louis...

Snap, snap, BANG... Shit!

It's happened, it's gone all through me, I feel it coming down; I can feel it coming out... I thought I could hold on but no, I've shat myself.

SHEILA

Things to always remember:

1) Smile. They like to see you enjoying it.
2) Take pride in your appearance, it's important to look good: hair, eyebrows, nails etc., they like that too.
3) Be firm but fair, but mainly firm – don't let them take the piss.
4) Adopt a zero-tolerance approach to those not wanting to pay. (It's your livelihood after all.)
5) Always remember why you're doing it. Always remember why.

Five rules I've learned in my first five months on the job. It's obviously hard to stick to all five on a single shift, but I've found it a good checklist to follow so far, and touch wood, fingers crossed, cross my heart and hope to die, it will continue to serve me well for the rest of my career behind the wheel, especially today.

But something doesn't quite feel right, what's that man holding in his hand? And why is he just standing here, right next to me, with his rucksack slung on his back like that? I'm tempted to look properly but I must keep my focus, keep my eyes on the road, I must not hit any kerbs or cyclists or children. I could alert the garage that I think something is wrong, but what kind of weak driver would that make me, on a big day like this too? It's probably nothing. I just have to drive on along Kingsland Road, remembering rules one, three and five. I can't let this lunatic ruin my big day, Hackney's big day.

My five golden rules are written out on the back of an old bus ticket I keep folded in my purse. The bus ticket is from my first day driving the 388 from Elephant and Castle to Stratford City. I remember it well, driving down Bethnal Green Road for the first time like I was edging down the streets of New Delhi, dazzled by the saris and sandals, and henna on hands and the overwhelming smell of spices. Since those early days, soaking up London life from my little cab at the front, I've kept my head down and really applied myself to do what it takes to be the capital's best bus driver. I've navigated last-minute diversions down narrow side streets, rowdy schoolkids, issues with zip cards and freedom passes, near misses with just about everything on wheels, whatever has been thrown my way, I'm managed it all, and with a smile too. Rule One.

And nearly six months in, it can't have really gone much better. What an honour it was to be called into the office last Friday and told the good news. The week before, while on my usual morning duty, someone from head office, disguised as a difficult passenger, was impressed with my route knowledge, the advice I gave, and the overall manner of my driving when I picked him up on Shoreditch High Street and dropped him off in Hackney Wick. It was reported that I 'drove exceptionally confidently with an infectiously friendly face' and was 'a real asset to the company'. Chris, the garage manager with the over-hanging belly of a beer-guzzling football hooligan, also told me, with remnants of leftover Bolognese still around his mouth from lunch, that I had received the most positive feedback from the *Comments, complaints and suggestions* sticker inside all of the buses. And with all things considered, he continued, panting heavily with the exhaustion of speaking, I was the perfect candidate for the launch of the brand new 392.

With this job, it finally feels like I'm on the right route and I couldn't be happier, I'm definitely more driven now. I'm happy. I even sometimes give my passengers little names as they get on: *cheers darling, thank you gorgeous, you're welcome hunnybunch*, you know, that sort of thing. Nearly all the passengers love it. You can see it on their face; it makes them feel good. For me, a bus journey should be an experience, so I make it my job to make sure that they're enjoying themselves, make existence a bit more bearable.

I've done my homework of course. This brand new Optare Solo midi has just twenty-five seats, with room for seven to stand if there aren't any wheelchairs or prams, or in today's case a three-team BBC London crew on board. It's not the youngest model you'll find on London's streets but it's small and nippy, and perfect for this little route. The running time is only thirty-six minutes (during peak hours). There are fixed bus stops most of the way, but a hail-and-ride section sometimes too, meaning people can get on and off when they want. There is already talk of a future northbound extension to Holloway Road Station, but I can't picture that prospect yet. I must navigate my way to Highbury safely, having been given the responsibility of driving this route on its first day of operation. I have to pace myself, contain it, excitement and speed.

Because this bus is so small, far smaller than the double-deckers I'm used to driving, I dreamt of a unity between us, like driving a people-carrier. I imagined passengers joking with each other, making friends and taking selfies. Instead, it feels odd, divided. Tension lives in the air like a bad smell, something chemical. Plus, the man at the front, who has been on since Hoxton, is still just standing there, in the way with his rucksack half on obstructing my left mirror, brazenly ignoring the sticker behind me which reads *Passengers must not stand beyond this point*. I can just about manage to see around him when I need to, but I know I should really say something.

There's another passenger, white and well-dressed sat window-side who hasn't stopped staring in my direction since he got on. His face looks red and agitated and I'm sure there is some movement in his trousers, a twitching down below he's trying to hide with his camel coat. He keeps fiddling with his privates and I can't help but feel distracted by his shamelessness.

The sky darkens and rain begins to fall; the road ahead looks grey and murky. The man still just stands there, gripping the yellow bar in front of him, eyes fixed forward. He is awkwardly positioned, passengers getting on have to squeeze past him and his bulky rucksack so they can touch in to pay. Passengers except for the granny with the trolley, who, despite Rule Four, I allow on without her pass – she'd lost it and I felt sorry for her.

As I cross Balls Pond Road into Midway Park, pulling up outside the library, there's an interaction I only half see, a conversation I only half hear, accusations fly about like shrapnel. I don't want this day to be tarnished by a silly spat; I don't want a disagreement to overshadow this special occasion. And then, as voices are raised higher, it dawns on me what someone is suggesting. They think the man, just inches from me, with the black beard, brown skin and big bag is some sort of terrorist.

A terrorist?

Maybe I can save this if I get to Highbury quickly enough. I pull out from the bus stop at speed. The rain is falling hard now. Rubber slides along the tarmac, grip slowly lost. The engine roars. I overtake a 21 at speed. There's a cyclist emerging from a side road on the left – a redhead. Knock down ginger? Left onto Newington Green with people working away on their MacBooks from the comfort of a cosy café. Strange man with bag still standing there. The mixture of fancy houses and council flats on Beresford Road. Man still there, still something black in his hand. Petherton Road. Mini-roundabout. Are... we... going... to... die? The Snooty Fox. The tiny Canonbury Station with its narrow entrance and bright orange signage. The suspect sneezes – no *bless yous* though. So nearly there. Get the remaining passengers to school, to work, to the shops safely and it's job done. Just a few more corners to navigate: Wallace Road, St. Paul's Road, Highbury Corner, third exit... last stop, the magistrates' court.

Three stops to go. Time: 9:37. Man with bag (potential bomb) still imminent threat. I slow a little for that sneaky speed camera, not that it matters now, then speed up again, fast. My duty card flaps about in the breeze. The morning traffic is heavy but the bus lane is free. A bell is rung. The lights stay green as I whizz past the Alwyne Castle and pull in behind a 30. The doors open but no one moves, everyone is still, facing the front like diligent school children. The rain falls faster. Weighty drops showering down like tears. The windscreen wipers swish left, swish right.

I close the doors and go again. I overtake. Two stops to go. It's getting harder to concentrate, keep my eyes on the road, see through the rain, see around the man. The schoolgirls are quiet. The old lady looks worried. The schoolboy and the sad-looking woman look like they're holding hands. The blind man, who moved away from the crackhead taking pictures with his invisible camera, looks uneasy. The MP is chewing on his fingernails and yanking on a piece of dead skin nervously. I can't see the faces of the camera crew, but I can imagine them. The mood is tense: fingers grip bag straps, palms clutch poles, it's all too quiet. I pull in quickly without indicating, braking a little too sharply to a stop, heads jerk forward and back again altogether as I apply the handbrake and exhale, mumbling a few hopeful words under my breath. Then, as I open the doors, at this the penultimate bus stop of the journey, Bus Stop D St. Pauls Road/Highbury & Islington Station, something strange happens. Something so totally unexpected and shocking by any account that I'm sure none of us can quite believe it. The man at the front, the strange man: brown face, big beard, green jacket, baggy denim jeans, rucksack over one shoulder, shifty, suspicious, a suspect, different, Muslim, terrorist, whatever you want to call him – with just one stop till the end of the route – goes to get off. I watch him, stunned, as he moves towards the open door of the bus and prepares to disembark: no explosives, no knives, no dead bodies, no news reports, no fireworks, no so-called Islamic State, nothing. Just another man, another Londoner, using public transport to go about his business: to work, to see a friend, to study, to grind and graft, to pay the bills, to treat themselves to something nice finally, normal things that you have to do in this beautifully difficult city.

'*Thank you driver,*' he says, turning towards me briefly, calmly, considerately. His eyes soft and submissive.

In his hand, seen clearly now, a small black phone, the shape and size of an old Nokia, clutched delicately in his palm as if clutching an orphaned bird. Despite the heavy rain, he steps off casually, looks right, then left, hitches his heavy rucksack over both shoulders and strolls back towards the direction of Canonbury. In my now unobscured left mirror, I see him stride past Sainsbury's, getting smaller and smaller, unprotected – no hat or umbrella – till he's disappeared completely. Perhaps, I see him veer right into a little side road.

There is a collective sigh as we eye the man out of view. Everything and everyone is calm. Craned necks turn back into place. Rain falls hard on the bus roof. Everyone looks towards me, and then around at each other, and through the mirror I look at all of them. The granny with the trolley is smiling, the suited black man with the satchel laughs, the blind man is shaking his head disbelievingly – someone must have told him. Maybe he can feel it. Feel that everything is alright now. The unity I dreamt of, finally achieved. I shake my head a little too, closing the doors to complete the final leg of the route. Across the road, a pretty blonde, a twenty-something City worker, smart navy suit and Asics on her feet drops her purse in her haste to escape the rain. An aging African, Ghanaian maybe, generic cleaning uniform, raincoat included, waddles after her. A tap on the shoulder does it. The exchange is brief. Business-like. These are not the conditions for pleasantries. A stifled *'thank you'*, before they both dart off to catch the Victoria Line.

Rule One. I can put my foot down now, enjoy this last bit, take it all in: the restaurants, that pub with the little theatre upstairs, the chicken and the charity shops, the people, the passengers, the workers, the parents, the truants. One stop to go, but now I don't want this journey to end. There's a 263 coming the other way, extended back to Highbury Barn again to make room for our arrival at the bus stand outside the court. They'll all be waiting for us. With a wide smile I force my way out in front of an Uber approaching Highbury Corner at speed with the road surface worsening, when, in the inside mirror, I spot something. Under a seat. The engine roars. I'm straining to see. The needle hits thirty, turns to forty and rises. The crackhead is still laughing his head off, the blind man is cackling to himself, the suited passenger with the stain on his trousers does a little jig. The back wheels skid. The laughing stops and the dancing is paused when *everyone* spots it, under the legs of one of the seats, a big black bag.

TONI

It took me ages to get these new white shirts and not bein' funny, don't wanna get blood on 'em now. Have you ever tried washin' blood off your clean clothes? Trust me, it's harder when it's not yours. I mean, at the end of the day, it's like gold dust gettin' a new uniform, so I'm not takin' any chances gettin' these dirty. It's gloves on, sleeves up, and get stuck right in while the adrenalin's goin'.

My friends think I've got it lucky, you know, workin' round here, but they don't know the half of it. Islington ain't that posh, definitely not as posh as people think. Yeah there's theatres and fancy bars and a Costa on every corner but you got the really rich and the really poor basically just livin' next-door to each other and that's been a real bad mix lately.

I've been on the force five years now. It's all I've ever wanted to do. In the Met, you've got to grow up fast. I'm at that stage now where I don't need anyone to talk me through anythin' anymore or hold my hand like I'm a little girl, I've seen it all. Don't need anybody to take it slow and explain the steps in a calm voice like I'm the baby of the force no more. I'm not no young officer fresh out of sixth form. I won't turn green. I won't turn around and start throwin' my guts up at the sight of a bit of blood because I'm a proper strong police officer, who's been there, done that, and for now, got the white shirts to prove it.

Yeah of course it's hard bein' a woman in this job sometimes. The fellas we nick definitely try and intimidate you; they'll say shit like they'll headbutt you or bite your fingers off or finger you in your sleep or somethin' but it's all just words, ain't it? Empty threats. I've heard them all before believe me. When you're bein' pushed against a wall or a shopfront or havin' your head forced to the ground by someone like me, you say things you don't mean 'cos you're angry and trapped and scared and embarrassed. I get that, trust me I do. Especially if your mates are watchin' from the side, or your family, wife and kids are shoutin' and screamin' and that. It's never nothin' personal though, I've just got a job to do. I might only be five-foot-four but I'm small and mighty like one of them Persil tablets you put in the wash. I just wanna catch the bad guys and keep Islington safe, keep London safe, that's all.

I still get that buzz you know. When a good call comes through and the blue lights go on, your body sort of shivers into action. All your senses are sharpened and a button inside you is suddenly switched on, because your brain knows somethin' has happened and you gotta do somethin' about it. The adrenalin is released and you gotta react. I can't really explain it. All I know is I love the thrill of it. There's somethin' about this city, it's always bubblin' under the surface, threatenin' to boil over without it ever actually happenin'. There's just enough bodies, just enough police officers or doctors or teachers or whatever to stop somethin' really, really bad from spillin' out of control. And that's London life, always on the edge. You're always just around the corner from somethin' excitin' or somethin' criminal or somethin' beautiful.

It's chocka. Traffic is buildin' up already headin' down to Highbury Corner. There are buses all in the bus lane not movin', some drivers are out of their vehicles tryin' to see what's causin' the hold-up. We speed down the other side of the road. We're doin' forty-five past Zia Lucia and N7 Vagabond and The Barn and The House of Hammerton and Bird and Jack Knife. Shops that didn't even exist half a decade ago. Tesco to the right. Little Waitrose to the left. A Majestic. As we get closer, it's obvious that this is a bad one. There's worry on people's faces, there's a cluster of people outside the magistrates' court, all wet and huddled together on their phones, people in hi-viz and people in suits and photographers, like they're waitin' for the arrival of somethin' that doesn't look like comin' anytime soon. Chris weaves in-between the stationary cars, the steerin' wheel is spinnin' left, then spinnin' right. His face is all pink and sweaty. It's completely gridlocked up ahead; more roadworks on Highbury Corner again aren't helpin'.

We edge forward, squeezin' between a double-decker 43 and a white delivery van. Chris honks the horn and I wind down the window and yell at a Prius to get out of the way. I can't even see beyond the traffic yet but I can sense somethin' very wrong. I look at Chris and even he, who has seen it all down the years, looks worried as he mutters a *fucking hell* under his breath when a cyclist pulls out dangerously from the left. With some quick thinkin', he mounts the pavement, weaves in-between the roadworks and the *Skanska* signs and wiggles free. It's not an ideal move but this is a critical situation. We overtake a few stationary cars and climb down from the kerb with a hefty bump by the Marie Curie on the corner. We're the first unit here it seems as we screech to a stop outside Hen and Chickens.

My eyes can't quite take in the scale of the scene as we pull up. Chris cuts the sound of the sirens but keeps the blue lights flashin' as we brace ourselves for what we'll see when we step out. The downpour is makin' it hard to pick out the particulars at first. I grab my hat from the dashboard and slide out the car in the heavy rain, with a heavy heart, and try to take in what has happened. The air's thick and clammy; I spot drops of blood on the concrete and debris strewn all over the ground, bits of bus and smashed glass. It's hard to see it all at once and for a moment my head's all over the place, I feel dizzy and sick, but when I do sort of get it together after a second a two, I'm sure I can make out bloodied bodies and two broken buses, one merged into the other. The damage suggests the single-decker swiped into the side of the double-decker at speed but it's hard to say, it's hard to see. I do the maths, tally up the sums: put one and one together, and get a number of casualties. All that's left is a shell of a bus, a little bus crushed in on itself, a crumpled mess, a wreck of a vehicle, destroyed and almost unrecognisable and a wounded double-decker that's been completely wiped out.

My heart's racin' and the funny smell in the air makes me cough so I'm forced to cover my mouth with my sleeve. I rush straight for the single-decker – what's left of it – but then stop myself mid-stride knowin' I probably shouldn't get any closer; there's protocol to follow. I should probably start cordonin' off the scene or somethin'. I should really wait for the fire crew, the paramedics, forensics and all the experts to sort out this massive mess, but what if there are people on board too injured to move? What if they need my help and I can save them before it's too late? I wouldn't be able to live with myself if I sat back and potentially let the death toll rise. I look at Chris and he's thinkin' the same but he gives me a look that says we should do what we can, while we can. My brain weighs up the pros and cons and eventually, against my better judgement, I edge closer armed with my torch and a fresh wave of adrenalin.

The rainwater gathered from my hat falls to the ground in heavy clumps. I run around the remains of the single-decker, the number 392 it says to the rear, skippin' over the puddles of blood mixed with rain. The engine which sits at the back, still mostly intact, is whinin' loudly, as if in pain. The only set of doors at the front has crushed in on impact and the roof has been bent out of shape. I climb through what was a window, glass crushin' under my boots as I plant my feet inside. I tread on and nearly trip over a bag – big and black, unscathed by the impact of the crash. Once in, it's a sorry sight, tangled wires and twisted limbs. Among the mangled yellow poles that look like broken yellow bones, I see a poor old lady, eighty odd, clutchin' a small black-and-white photo. I kneel down to look at the picture more closely but the image has been smudged, so the darker figure, her husband I presume, is hard to make out. She lies there in a pool of blood, the photograph slowly escapin' her grasp.

I spot two schoolgirls in Highbury Fields uniforms, stuck together like Siamese twins, two halves of one whole. I see a football fan, in a shirt of a team I half recognise, an open wound to the head, restin' his pale white hand on the chest of a big black male. All of them with life-changin' injuries. I wouldn't call myself religious or anythin' but

The 392

I find myself touchin' the centre of my forehead, then my chest, then my left shoulder, then my right one and whisperin' 'Amen' under my breath. It seems like the right thing to do.

I scan what's left, lookin' over my shoulder at the blood, the bodies, the broken bus all in bits. The front of the single-decker has sort of crumpled in on itself, surface area halved. I picture what might have happened and try to play the scene over in my head like it's the last bit of a film and all the passengers are characters. I've seen enough traffic incidents to know the signs: who the victims are, who's usually to blame, how the collision happened, but my brain feels funny tryin' to piece this broken puzzle together, it's a tricky one, there are definitely pieces missin'. I think I might know how, but I can't work out why this has happened.

Chris is behind me, there on the radio tryin' to report everythin' he sees back to the station, knelt down over an injured body, anglin' his shoulder and speakin' into it, tryin' to stay calm but even he's rattled. He steps off the bus, holdin' his head and lookin' desperate for air. I shuffle right, hoist my right leg over the debris, left one follows, hurdlin' limbs and hunks of headlight. I hear panicked voices and cries outside, and sirens approachin' in the distance. The voices seem to be gettin' closer and closer like they're comin' from the bus itself. There's clearly not much I can do now so I consider gettin' off before the experts come and cordon off the scene but then I hear a soft voice from behind me, someone stirrin' themselves awake, a fighter.

'Boxer,' a little voice says groggily. I turn around to see an injured young woman holdin' her stomach and wincin'. 'Boxer, wake up.' Her voice is brittle and broken and she's covered in dust as she stretches out to touch the chest of a young boy, his body in a heap. She's hurt but he's worse. She's wearin' a leather jacket that's been ripped apart from under the right arm. There is blood on her but I can't see the source of the wound. She shifts her weight right and shuffles closer to the young boy in the ragged school uniform. I don't think she's seen me yet through the wreck, dallyin' awkwardly in what was the aisle of the bus, as she struggles to prop herself up. She pushes away a large bit of plastic off her legs and tries nudgin' the boy awake. 'Boxer, come on get up, it's me Natalie.'

She's clearly hurt so I intervene. 'Stay there I'm comin',' I call out, but she barely acknowledges me as I climb over a broken seat and negotiate my way through the mess towards her. As I do, I catch my trouser leg on the sharp end of a broken bit of glass. The pointy bit rips through the fabric and scratches the surface of my skin. I feel the blood begin to ooze out and run down my leg.

'Boxer... wake up!' The young girl is shakin' the boy now, urgin' him to open his eyes and breathe again. She moves her face closer to his and softly kisses his face and neck. 'Please

Boxer,' she pleads, her voice desperate and unsteady. She holds his left hand; he remains completely still. I hear her sob and soon after see the tears roll down her cheek and fall from her sweet brown eyes onto his dusty brown skin. She cradles the boy like he's an infant, like one of them mothers from those charity adverts shot in Africa for *Comic Relief*. There are specs of red in his afro. I see the death of a young black teenager on the streets of north London at least every other week in this job but her tears make this the saddest.

I suddenly notice as I look right, facin' the front end of this bus, a man, six-foot-nothin'-ish, who has apparently appeared from nowhere. Alarmed by his presence, I instinctively reach for my taser, but hesitate to draw and aim it immediately. I imagine he has forced his way through, forced his way on, clambered over a smashed window, he looks determined to do somethin'. He's drippin' with rainwater but doesn't bother wipin' himself dry. I eye him up and down cautiously. Take everythin' in. Black trainers, white sole, no name, loose-fittin' denim jeans with no distinctive markin' or pattern. He selflessly begins yankin' at large bits of bus and shovin' things out the way like it's rubble from some war-torn country. There's a resilience in his nature, a desire to help. His method is unconventional, showin' little care for the evidence and investigation to follow but that doesn't matter, I admire his relentlessness. He pauses, puffs out his cheeks and looks at the damage then continues pushin' aside bits of metal to try and retrieve the poor people. He has his rucksack on, both straps, brand: No Fear.

'Sir, you must vacate the scene immediately,' my voice sounds harsher than it should be, must be the shock. He's clearly tryin' to help, but there's protocol to follow.

'This could've been me… I was just on this bus, I heard the crash and ran back, I must help them.' There is a strong sadness in his face, a desire to make things better.

'Sir, I really must insist. You must leave now.' I release the grip on my taser and grab his shoulders. Chris watches closely through a smashed window as I usher the man towards a gap where the door was but he jerks back forcefully, aggressively almost, which startles me.

He then grabs me by my arms and sternly says, 'No. I must help. These people need help.'

The sirens are louder now; the other units must be close. Soon I will be stood down, told to go back to the station and offered a cup of tea with lots of sugar for the shock. I will have to write a lengthy statement and then be told to go home early and rest up after the crazy day I've had. It's mad because, when you think about all the normal things that happen on a normal bus journey, this weren't meant to happen. A bus journey is just meant to be one of those things that you have to put up with even when you don't really want to, like goin' to the bank. It's necessary once in a while.

I don't usually take the bus, but I know what it's like and

this weren't meant to happen. You know, you wait, the time on the countdown thing at the bus stop is wrong and it's pissin' it down (it's always pissin' it down) and you don't believe in umbrellas. And as every second goes by, you don't believe in buses, as the rain soaks into your shoes, you definitely don't believe in buses. It's at times like these you picture yourself in Marbella, or the Caribbean or Mexico, on a nice beach somewhere gettin' a tan, but instead you open your eyes and see a Poundland and a Lidl and remember you're in Ilford. Five minutes pass. Then, ten. Every bus comes, except yours and you think about ringin' in and pullin' a sickie because you would rather be in bed with a cup of tea and some choccy biscuits watchin' *Homes Under The Hammer*, but then the bloody bus comes at last and bursts your balloon before it's even fully blown. You're soakin' wet before you even get on. Someone who's only been waitin' a few minutes rudely pushes on first and you're too tired to even argue with him so you just give him a dirty look that he doesn't understand. The driver doesn't smile and your card doesn't work first time and there are a pair of grannies in the seats at the front and their trolleys are half-blockin' the aisle. An African woman has taken off her shoes and is flexin' her feet and stretchin' out her calloused toes. There's a couple of black boys at the back slurpin' on tins of strawberry Nurishment. There's a man whose bag takes up a whole seat, and he doesn't even look like movin' it any time soon, he just looks through you and continues playin' a colourful game on his phone. He gives you a look that says *fuck off* in every sense so you don't even bother gettin' into an argument with him. You're lucky to find a seat but then you quickly realise the fella next to you stinks and you feel bad if you move now so you hold your breath until one of you gets off. But you both stay on till the end, and the stench gives you a migraine and it's not even ten yet.

The rain stops, it always does once you're inside but the glass of the window is steamin' up so you can't even see out properly. And there's this nasty guy standin' in the buggy area coughin' his lungs up and not coverin' his mouth; you can actually see the germs flyin' about around the bus. And there's this other guy diggin' inside his nose then thinkin' whether or not to eat what he has found up there. He has a little look around to see if anyone is lookin' at him, or in his general direction, and then shoves it right in his gob. And the bus is freezin', it's always bloody freezin', and the schoolkids are bein' noisy and playin' crap music off their phones. The traffic is heavy and the bus stops for a long time at a bus stop for no reason 'cos nobody gets on or off and there's an argument startin' at the front because someone isn't movin' down. The smell gets worse and you're runnin' late for mornin' briefin', and wolfin' down breakfast this mornin' has made your belly feel funny. This, all of this, is meant to happen because this is what bus journeys in London are like. And a little bit later than you wanted, you force your way off, breathe in the smoggy

The 392

London air, enter the station and go about your day and forget about what the bus journey was like this mornin', because no matter how unenjoyable it was, nothin' *that* terrible happened. But this, this scene right here, in the middle of Islington, this weren't meant to happen. This weren't no normal journey.

ACKNOWLEDGEMENTS

I owe much of this cherished publication to my wonderful agent Philippa Sitters of David Godwin Associates for her radiant positivity on this journey from the start. Largely thanks to her, this little story has come a very long way.

Thank you to OWN IT!, Crystal Mahey-Morgan and Jason Morgan, for being independent and mighty. Their belief in me has made a young man's dream come true.

Thank you to my beautiful Elisabeth for her love and support and casting an editorial eye over these words over the course of the last few years. I don't think I could have done this without you, I am eternally grateful.

I would like to thank the students from St. Martin's-in-the-Fields High School for Girls and Hampstead School respectively for humouring me while I shared with them abridged snippets in our English lessons.

From City, University of London, I would like to thank tutor Clare Allan, mentor Jeremy Page and Dr. Patrick Brindle for their guidance and expertise in the early stages of the process. I would like to especially show my gratitude to Julie Wheelwright from City, whose ceaseless belief in my potential kept me going when things looked hairy.

Thank you to friends David Rank, Andy Wands, Cassey Williams and Nicolas Boyd for being super supportive throughout.

Next: thanks to Deborah Blake for being editor extraordinaire, and James Nunn for the truly arresting front cover.

Most importantly, I would to thank my loving family: my wonderful Mum, Nana, Pappy, Tyler, Dad, Grandad, Niah, Uncle Shaun and the rest of my wonderfully crazy blood relatives. R.I.P Nanny my favourite bus-ride companion. Love you lots, this one's for you too.

Big up all the bus drivers out there.

To everyone else, keep striving. Make your dreams come true.